AF481749

INSPIRATION
takes a
VACATION

An Epic Love Story

By
Annette Mori

Back of the Book

Abby Prentice is suffering through the worst writer's block in her entire career. After deciding to escape her home's confines, she takes a walk on the beach and meets a mysterious woman who, Abby believes, must be the reincarnation of Helen of Troy. After the strange woman claims that she is on vacation, Abby quickly offers her personal services as a tour guide. Evasive about where she lives and why she has chosen Forks, Washington, as the destination for her three-day vacation, the stranger is only mildly annoying to Abby.

Feeling burnt out, Musetta desperately needs a vacation. Her boss reluctantly agrees to three days. On the first day of her adventure, she is delighted to almost literally run into her favorite writer and begin her three-day adventure. As she spends more time with Abby, she finds it increasingly difficult to return to her job despite the catastrophic consequences of leaving her position. For the first time, Musetta is falling in love.

Soon into their journey, both women notice something odd is happening all around them. Abby is not the only writer experiencing a block. Art in every form has come to a screeching halt in the Northwest. The media is forecasting an end to cultured civilization, beauty, and emotion as we know it. Will the women find a way to return inspiration to the Northwest, and does Musetta have the key to solving the crisis?

Acknowledgments

A huge thank you to all of my beta readers: Gail Dodge, Carrie Camp, Ameliah Faith, Dana Holmes, Danna Micoletti, Emily Cubbage, McGee Mathews, and Erin Saluta, who made great suggestions to improve the initial draft.

I would also like to express my gratitude to McGee Mathews, who walked me through the self-publishing process to make this all possible.

Thanks to Angela Koenig for her magic as the final editor to tighten the story even further. She is a delight to work with. Huge thanks to all the other readers and fellow writers who have sent personal emails, written reviews, and posted nice things on Facebook (you know who you are). The Affinity authors are an especially supportive group and often share posts or send words of encouragement. Finally, my wife, Jody, continues her support even when it interferes with our time.

Dedication

To McGee Mathews, who freely gave me her time and expertise. And, as always, to my beautiful wife, whom I love with all my heart.

Also by Annette Mori

Novels

One Shot at Love
Heart Strings Attached with Ali Spooner
Pleasure Workers
Compound Interest
A Window to Love
Artist Free Zone
The Book Witch
The Book Addict
The Dream Catcher
Free to Love with Ali Spooner
Unconventional Lovers
The Organization with Erin O'Reilly
Captivated
The Termination
The Review
The Ultimate Betrayal
Locked Inside
Out of This World
Asset Management
Love Forever, Live Forever

Short Stories/Novellas

A Trophy Wives Christmas (With Ali Spooner) - Affinity's 2020 Charity

Donner Jr. Saves the Day - Affinity's 2020 Charity Anthology

Witches, Vampires, and Shifters, Oh My - Lady Grimm Anthology

The Forty-Year Old Virgin: A Lesbian Twist - Conference Call

Velvet's Guardian Angel - The Velvet Anthology

The Coochie Couch - Lonestar Anthology

We're Not in Kansas Anymore

The Thanksgiving Baby Caper

Who is Nicolas Claus - Christmas Medley 2017

Vampire Pussy…Cat - *It's in Her Kiss*, Affinity's Charity Anthology

Nicky's Christmas Miracle X3 - *It's in Her Kiss*, Affinity's Charity Anthology

The Incredibly True Adventure of Two Elves in Love - Affinity 2014 Christmas

The True Story of Valentine's Day

Table of Contents

PROLOGUE

The Nine Muses of Greek Mythology

The sisters, his daughters, were bickering again. They sounded more like human children, not the ancients, and certainly not like the nine muses. If Zeus hadn't wanted to hear what they were saying, he would have stopped them. Instead, he listened in on their argument.

"I blame you, Calliope, and you're no better, Erato, with your notions of love. If you'd only had your fling with a woman, none of this would be happening," Melpomene chastised.

"I disagree. Where would we have been when the artists inevitably multiplied had it not been for our offspring?" Erato defended.

"Of course you would take Calliope's side in this matter. The two of you have always banded together. History is repeating itself. It's no wonder past events influenced

Musetta. She has not one but two indiscretions to overcome in her 'family' history. That has weakened our strength. It's no wonder Musetta is experiencing problems. Inspiration taking a vacation. Preposterous. You have acted like animals in heat. We could have covered all the territories," Melpomene argued.

"Bull. Tragedy swirls all around. That's all you see. The real tragedy would have been ignoring what was right in front of us. We needed to involve the humans. Erato's choice was a poet, and his blood runs through her daughters. That has been a good thing," Calliope insisted. "I refuse to listen to you prattle on. This temporary hiccup will work out as it's supposed to. Musetta is obsessed with a woman, not a man. This won't be the same, and you know it. Have you forgotten Sappho? Erato took a special interest in Sappho before Zeus blessed Erato's marriage to Malos. Surely Sappho would not have found a special place in history had it not been for Erato."

Melpomene made a brushing motion with her hand as if to wipe away an annoying insect. "You had your pick of acceptable mates—both of you. I can assure you that my mate is passionate enough. There was no need to seek anything outside of the acceptable boundaries."

Euterpe's musical voice entered the fray. "To be fair, aren't you forgetting Mnemosyne, our mother?"

Melpomene pointed her nose in the air. "She had the good sense to leave us with Apollo and Eufime, where thankfully Apollo provided his wisdom and guidance. None of us had any interest in the boring day-to-day drudgery our mother endured. Even you, Calliope, and you, Erato, lacked interest until puberty. As I said before, rutting like animals.

At least Mnemosyne fell under a god's charms. That, I understand."

"You sully our mother's good name. Father will have something to say about that. He's never been too concerned with what has happened. What is done is done. We need to move forward, not back. I don't believe our daughters have performed with any less distinction than your own, despite your haughty view of their ancestry. Calliope, go to him and ask for an audience before Musetta takes it upon herself to make the plea. Zeus will listen to you." Erato touched her sister's shoulder in support.

Calliope nodded. "It's the least I can do for her. I wish I had done more for Dumi when I had the chance."

Zeus didn't need to hear any more. This rift was not good. At some point, he would need to intervene because he knew the issue would arise again. Calliope and Erato had cemented that long ago when they'd chosen human lovers. He would listen because both sides had valid perspectives. He needed to remember that as he weighed his options. After all, he was the boss.

CHAPTER ONE

Abigail Prentice had holed up in her tiny apartment for the past seven days. At least she'd graduated to showering every day. She'd engrossed herself in several television marathons—Netflix, Apple TV, Amazon Prime, anything to avoid her laptop. Abby imagined the damn thing glaring at her or the blinking screen simulating how a computer might telegraph hurt. If she was honest with herself, lately, the ghostly white glare reminded her of a cheap horror flick—a blinding light on her utterly blank manuscript.

In her head, she thought of what her laptop might say to her. "Why are you avoiding me again? You know how much I love it when your fingers dance across my keyboard."

When Abby wasn't spending her free time binge-watching the different shows, she posted cat videos on Facebook or slipped in random comments to posts already taking on a life of their own.

Danger lurked around every corner for Abby, which was why she thought a writer was the safest occupation she could have chosen. Unfortunately, she was in the midst of the most prolonged dry spell of her entire career. She hadn't written a single fictional word in over three months. She'd joked on Facebook that inspiration had taken a sabbatical, and she wasn't sure the persnickety woman was coming back.

"Screw it," she muttered and flung the covers aside. After setting her iPad on the glass table, Abby shuffled into the bathroom and began brushing her teeth. *What good does it do to live in such a beautiful place if I never leave my bedroom?*

Peeking through the blinds, she was happy to see a tiny patch of blue sky far in the distance through the tall trees. Once the fog lifted, the beach might be a safe place to try to get back her writing mojo. Hadn't she always heard that's where writers teased forth their inspiration? How dangerous could it be to take a walk on the beach and clear her head from those maudlin thoughts? Lately, she'd wondered if she'd ever write another word. Although writing was in her blood, she didn't worry about losing income. She had enough to retire if she wanted to.

Abby supposed she fit the stereotype of an eccentric writer. Single woman, living alone with her cat. If a person looked in the dictionary next to the word *recluse*, she imagined her mugshot would stare back at them. Sure, she was friendly with the locals because she didn't completely lack social skills. Once she had her best friend, Jenny, and Jenny's daughter, Nat, to hang with. Unfortunately, rather than literally plummeting, she'd fallen for Jenny and had an epic crash and burn. They weren't talking to one another at the moment. No one had to tell her it was a bad idea to be in love with your straight best friend.

Abby replayed the conversation she'd had with Jenny. The night had been perfect before her confession. Nat was at work, and Jenny had invited her over for dinner. She'd said she wanted to tell her something important. Abby had misread the cues. She was all smiles when Abby had arrived with pie and ice cream. After dinner, they'd sat close together on the couch, and Abby had jumped at the chance to tell her how she felt.

Jenny looked so good. She had such a glow about her that night, so Abby had blurted, "I'm in love with you, Jenny. I have been for a long time, but of course, I couldn't tell you when you were still married."

The smile slipped from Jenny's face, and the small crinkle on her brow deepened. She sucked in a mouthful of air before responding.

"Abby, you're my best friend in the whole world. I would like nothing better than to fall madly in love with you. I love you with all my heart. But there isn't the tiniest bit of gayness in any bone in my body. I'm so sorry. I wish I were a lesbian or bisexual because I can't think of a better partner or coparent for Nat, even though she's all grown now."

"Oh," Abby barely whispered. "Well, this is awkward," she added as her body moved of its own accord several feet from Jenny.

"It doesn't have to be awkward. I'm sure we'll laugh this off in a few months. Besides, you can do way better than an old divorcee with a daughter ready to start college."

Abby stood abruptly, bumping her knee against the coffee table. "Shit," she exclaimed. "Um, it's late. I better go now."

Jenny touched Abby's arm. "Abs, don't go. We should talk about this."

"I can't. Give me a little time, please?" Tears pricked at the corner of her eyes.

"Okay, if that's what you need. I know you like to process things on your own. Don't take too long." Jenny reached for Abby to embrace her, and selfishly, Abby melted into the hug, knowing it meant something very different to Jenny.

The first two months following the disaster had resulted in isolation and questionable hygiene. With everything except her writing, Abby believed she had started to turn a corner.

As quickly as the memory surfaced, Abby swallowed it down. No backtracking. She refused to let those feelings make matters worse than they already were. Shouldn't heartbreak be an inspiration for a perfect romance novel?

She smiled when Plato, her orange tabby, trotted along behind her. He liked to follow her everywhere she went. In the middle of the night, this meant disaster. Four broken toes, a concussion, and too many bruises to count did not convince Abby that Plato was hazardous to her health. She needed someone to cuddle with at night, and the price for that comfort was not too high for her to pay.

"Plato, can you please give Mommy a little space? If I trip over you, I won't be able to walk the beach and find inspiration. I wish that slippery little bugger would turn out to be a beautiful woman." Abigail chuckled at her lame joke.

"Meow."

"Yeah, keep meowing, will you? At least then I'll know where you're at and can avoid another unfortunate mishap."

"Meow."

Even though it was summer, the chill in the morning air was enough to warrant a bulky sweatshirt or light jacket. Sometimes the fog would hang in the air, reluctant to dissipate before noon, even with the persistence of sunshine in the distance. Abby thought the mist that often appeared in the Pacific Northwest was like a desperate beauty queen—unwilling to let go despite the telltale signs of aging.

Looking in the mirror, she saw evidence of the passing of time. She stuck her tongue out at her reflection. It was such a childish thing to do but gave her immense pleasure. Lately, she'd moved closer to the mirror to inspect the fine lines around the corners of her eyes. Bit by bit, year by year, she was losing her youthful appearance. If she didn't put herself out there, she was destined for the label of crazy cat lady.

Selecting the warmest sweatshirt, she pulled the soft fabric over her head and stepped into the chill of the morning air. A small shiver traveled over her body before she began the brisk walk to the beach. Soon, she was warm enough to feel the beginnings of perspiration underneath her protective clothing. Abby debated whether she should stop and remove her sweatshirt but thought better of it, knowing once she hit the beach and sat on a log, she would feel the crispness of the air. Then again, if she didn't, her sweat would turn into a damp cold and burrow inside like an intruder. Unwelcome. Uncomfortable.

Walking close to the water, the wind whipped fiercely across Abby's face. Her long brown hair kept slapping against her skin and sticking to the corners of her full lips. Her slim fingers continued to push her hair behind her ears. Eating her long strands was not her idea of a good time. The sting of her thick locks against her cheeks wasn't pleasant either. She chastised herself for not bringing something to tie back the offending tresses. Bending her head, she attempted to keep the wind from doing more damage.

It shouldn't have been a surprise that she found herself in a face-plant spitting out a mouthful of wet sand. The bacteria in the sand would probably end up causing a fatal illness.

What was unexpected were the two shapely legs less than a yard from where she was unceremoniously spewing the gritty substance.

A magnetic pull caused her to stop the purge as her eyes traveled to a sheer white coverall that barely hid the voluptuous body concealed beneath. The practical side of Abby thought that the swimsuit cover was utterly inadequate for the day's weather. Another thought, undeniably salacious, was how easily the wind would cause the coverall to reveal the woman's ample breasts. *Please let her swimsuit be as skimpy as a boutique dares to sell.*

Abby's eyes finally landed on the face she believed must belong to a living, breathing, Helen of Troy. Her long blonde hair fell softly across her shoulders in gentle waves. Dark black lashes framed her almost translucent blue eyes. Her generous cupid's bow mouth looked like Leonardo da Vinci had painted it on himself. Almost as if a hidden force compelled her, Abigail looked to her left, sure she would see those famed thousand ships.

"Are you injured?" the velvety voice asked. The stranger's voice had the kind of calming quality that could tease a frightened animal from its hiding place.

Abby was that frightened animal. Right from the start, she was coaxed from her awkward hiding place. She quickly stood, brushing the sand from her clothes. She pushed back her long hair, currently obscuring her view of the woman standing in front of her. The woman's head was slightly cocked to the side.

"Oh yeah, yeah. I fall all the time. I'm like the Olympic Gold favorite in the *falling-on-sand* sport." Groaning at her inane response, she failed to resist adding a ridiculous question to the end of the first words out of her mouth. "Aren't you cold?"

The woman's mirth appeared on her face as a smile tugged ever so slowly at the corners of her naturally red lips. "Isn't this a beach? I have a swimming robe."

"Huh? Swimming robe? I suppose that's a good descriptor." Continuing to hold her hair away from her face, Abby squinted into the bright sun. "Um, we're not exactly on a beach in Southern California." Forging ahead, she added, "Your name wouldn't happen to be Helen, would it?"

Before the words left her mouth, she mentally slapped the side of her head. She was being ridiculous, her awkwardness spilling out in a tsunami wave. The woman's delicate laughter, fragile and beautiful like the wings of a butterfly, broke her silent chastising.

"No, my name is Musetta. It's an ancient name, but an appropriate name. You're the writer, Abigail Prentice. I'm very sorry, but I needed a vacation."

Abby's nose wrinkled. How the hell did this woman know her name? She wasn't that famous. Sure, there was a picture of her on every book, but she didn't believe many individuals would recognize her, not for one second.

The niggle of discomfort left Abby almost immediately because there was something about this woman that seemed vulnerable. She had the urge to pamper the stranger. Forget that she couldn't adequately nurture herself and barely managed to take care of her cat.

"Hmm, clearly you've never vacationed this far north. My place is within walking distance. Come with me. Perhaps a nice hot tea or cocoa will warm you up."

Puffing her cheeks and shaking her head, she kept her occasionally unkind thoughts about tourists to herself. *At least she doesn't seem to be the* Twilight-*craze type of person.* Even though it had been seven years since the last movie in the series was released, the hordes of *Twilight* fans returned each year for Bella's birthday celebration. Forks, Washington, was several miles away, but the tourists often made their way farther south to the beach. She didn't begrudge the town that short spike in their economy. It was needed.

"I wish to try this cocoa. That would be lovely. Thank you, Abigail Prentice, writer."

***

The short journey to Abby's quaint home near the water seemed a welcome relief to Musetta. Her shivering subsided to nearly nothing once the two women made it inside. Wind and the region's dampness always seemed to add to the chill, even in summer.

Musetta appeared to take in the small space in one polite glance as Abby led her to the overstuffed couch. It almost felt as though they were two old friends reconnecting after a few years of not seeing one another. Abby felt a jolt of anxiety at this thought. That was precisely what had happened over several years with her and her best friend, Jenny, until everything went sideways. She didn't want to go to that uncomfortable place—time to find out more about this mysterious woman.

"Please tell me you aren't one of those rabid *Twilight* fans. For whatever reason, you don't strike me as the type."

Musetta's pleasant chuckle filled the pockets of space in her house. Not that it was substantial, but the sparsity of furniture made for a lot of wide-open space.

"No, but I would like to think I had a small part in Stephenie's success."

"You know Stephenie Meyer?" Abby's eyes went wide in surprise.

"In a manner of speaking." The wry smile returned to Musetta's face. Not exactly mocking. It was something else entirely.

"Who are you?" This was a rhetorical question, but Abby found herself wanting to know more about the breathtaking woman who sat poised in front of her like a Greek goddess.

"I'm nobody. Simply a woman who wanted to experience life from the other side. Artists, particularly you, Abigail Prentice, are a fascination to me. I had to know why."

"The other side? Why?" Riddles. Abby wondered about the riddles. She enjoyed unraveling those in her books, but that was fantasy. She had an alarming amount of irritation about the pesky inconveniences to her organized and precise routines in real life. Her life was bland and predictable. She liked it that way. No conflict. No waves. And no unanswered questions. Even if those answers were not the ones she preferred hearing. Abby did not enjoy mystery in her meticulous, uneventful life.

Why does this strange woman keep using my first and last name? And, how the hell does she know me? The questions multiplied. Surely that photo on her books' covers was not the answer. *Is she an unstable fan? Does she drop my name much like Stephenie Meyer's, as if she personally knows the writer?*

"Don't be alarmed, Abigail Prentice."

"I'm not alarmed. Stop calling me Abigail Prentice. It's creepy, and that does not match your outward appearance or your lovely laughter. Call me Abby."

"Very well, Abby. Do you need a reminder to put the water on?" A glint of mischief appeared in Musetta's eyes. "I believe I would like a short name. You may call me Muse."

"Nickname." Abby shook her head. "No, the short name is more appropriate." Abby stood and walked to the kitchen to begin filling the teakettle. "Where are you from?"

"No particular place. I move around quite a bit. My territory spans the Pacific Northwest. I've been having a bit of a crisis lately and needed to take a break. Even though this holiday will further exacerbate my work, I hope that when I return, my subjects will have renewed interest."

"Cryptic much?"

There was that laughter again. The one that matched the power of Muse's beauty. Abby believed she would travel to Hell and back to hear Muse laugh again.

"In due time, Abby. In due time."

"Okay, if you won't tell me where you're from, how about telling me how you ended up in this remote part of the world if you aren't a *Twilight* fan? Unless you're a big fan of the rain, Forks isn't exactly a preferred holiday destination."

"I don't understand why not. There is beauty here. The Hoh Rainforest has a special charm. Isn't that why you chose to move here? You believed this place would bring you inspiration?"

A bitter laugh erupted from Abby. "Inspiration, ha. Right now, I'm cursing that stingy bitch."

The horror on Muse's face stopped Abby in her tracks. Running to soothe whatever she'd done to offend the woman caused her to trip and bang the top of her head. The crack against the glass table in front of her couch echoed in the room.

***

Abby opened her eyes and found her head cradled in the woman's lap as a rivulet of tears streamed down Muse's face. She couldn't figure out why Muse was crying, but Abby was sure she was the cause. *Why did I have to get the klutz gene from my father?*

"Oh, Abby, I'm sorry. So, so, sorry. Lately, I can't seem to do anything right."

"What? No, no, whatever I did to make you cry, I'm the one who should be apologizing." Abby reached up to touch her head, which had already started to throb. A sticky substance coated her fingers, and if she hadn't already been nearly on the ground, she would have returned. Blood. Abby did not do well with blood. The number of times she'd bled was too many to count. Her own or anyone else's brought an immediate wave of nausea. Fainting was a common occurrence.

"Your head requires first aid."

"Apparently, yes, it does. Um, don't freak if I hit the ground again." Abby started to rise and felt a gentle hand hold her in place while Muse managed to remove Abby's bleeding head from her lap.

"I'll get something to staunch the flow that obviously causes you so much distress."

"Okay." Abby groaned. She wanted to make a better impression, but the black cloud that seemed to follow her around would not dissipate for any reason. "It seems no matter what I do, clumsiness will not take a vacation. She seems to follow me around wherever I go. All my life, she's been my BFF. Too bad inspiration turned out to be a mean girl, and she's clearly whooping it up in Mexico."

It sounded like Muse was rummaging around in her bathroom. When she poked her head out, the crinkle in her brow was the most exaggerated expression of confusion Abby had ever seen. She almost looked like a cartoon character.

"No, not Mexico, and what a terrible thing to say. She is not a mean girl," Muse huffed.

"Sorry, it's just a joke. Why are you getting so—"

"After I fix your head, I'll be going. Clearly, you don't know how difficult it is to inspire so many for so long. Ungrateful artists…" Muse grumbled. She was carrying the first aid kit that Abby had stored in one of the drawers attached to the bath cabinet.

Abby began to sit up, and the woozy feeling was instantaneous, but it was important to understand why Muse appeared so irritated. "You're angry."

Muse halted her progress and stopped mid-stride. "I am." Her eyes widened, and then she smiled. "Such a human emotion, huh?"

"I'm not sure why you're angry, but I'm going to apologize again because I get the sense that somehow I'm the cause."

Muse squatted next to Abby as she opened the box and pulled a large piece of gauze from inside. Gently placing the absorbent fabric on the wound, she used more pressure, holding it in place for several seconds. "Let's see how much damage there is."

After Muse lifted the gauze, Abby found not having Muse's hand on her head was worse, even though the pressure had caused a tiny bit of pain.

"It probably looks more serious than it really is. Head wounds bleed a lot. Something to do with those blood vessels so close to the surface. There's a ton in a person's head."

"And you know this how?" The tiny smile left Abby with the impression that whatever had angered Muse was less of an issue at this moment.

"I asked the ER doctor once. I was curious and thought I might be able to use that fact in one of my stories. The first few times had really freaked me out, but then I figured heads bleed a lot, so I asked. He told me I should be more concerned about losing consciousness."

"The first few times? Is this a common occurrence?" Muse continued to pat the wound with care.

Abby shrugged. "Yeah. I tend to get hurt a lot. Mostly it's my own fault, but Plato contributes his fair share."

"Plato?"

"My cat. He insists on following me around unless I have company, and then Plato is the very definition of a scaredy-cat. He's hiding from you right now."

"That's unfortunate. I would have enjoyed meeting your companion. Your books often feature cats. The wound won't stop bleeding. I believe this will require stitches." She frowned as she moved closer to inspect the injury.

Abby pointed to the box. "Use the Super Glue. I got sick of going to the ER all the time, and I found out that Super Glue works just as well. Fortunately, I don't react negatively to whatever chemicals make up that little miracle. It's saved me a lot of money over the years. That and Steri-Strips. Those might work too."

"Surely you are not serious."

"I sure am. I can't afford my klutzy nature. I've adapted over the years." Abby plucked a new packet of gauze from the box, quickly opening it and pressing it on her forehead. She finally felt stable enough to stand and grab the glue with her other hand after tossing the packaging on the coffee table. She shoved the glue in her pocket.

"I'll do it. As soon as the blood flow stems, I can handle my own injuries."

"I don't think your wound has stopped bleeding."

Abby stood on wobbly legs and did her best to try to control her gait. Waving the gauze at Muse, she started for her bathroom. "I'll be fine. Just relax. This will only take a few minutes. Don't leave, please," she pleaded.

The minute Abby looked into the mirror and got her first glimpse of the dried blood mixing with a new stream of red continuing to flow freely down her face, Abby knew she wasn't going to remain upright. She didn't remember hitting the hard floor.

CHAPTER TWO

The woman was infuriating. Muse simply wanted a vacation. Needed a vacation. She'd told Zeus if he didn't let her do this, things would get a lot worse. He'd reluctantly agreed. But instead of relaxing on the beach and enjoying the rest she so desperately needed, Muse was tending to one of her most valuable subjects. *Subjects* might not be a very respectful name, but Muse didn't have a better one.

Waiting patiently for Abby to return to the small living area, Muse heard the loud thud. *Oh no, that can't be good.*

She rushed into the bathroom only to find Abby splayed across the hard tile floor. Blood continued to ooze from her previous injury, and Muse wondered if there would be a new source to attend to. The clean gauze lay to the right of her hand. Muse didn't believe the bandage was sterile anymore. Quickly returning to the living room, she grabbed another package of gauze, several alcohol swabs, and a tube of antibiotic ointment. She silently thanked Abby for having a well-stocked first aid kit.

First things first. Abby had insisted Super Glue would do the trick, so Muse figured it couldn't be that hard to fix the original cut. She would worry about any other injuries later.

Opening the gauze, Muse gently dabbed the gash and then used the alcohol wipes and antibiotic cream to clean the wound. When the blood flow started to subside, she began searching Abby's pockets for the glue.

"Unh," Abby groaned. "I don't think I know you well enough for you to be fumbling with my clothes." Abby's eyes fluttered open, and she blinked several times. "What are you doing?"

"Shh. Stop being so stubborn and let me play doctor or nurse."

A wolfish grin appeared on Abby's face, and Muse couldn't help smiling in return. "Playing doctor or nurse with an angel…yup right up there on my bucket fantasy list."

Muse had managed to find the glue and remove the cap. A quick dab at the wound eliminated the last droplets of blood. Muse adeptly used her fingers to close the gap in the cut and then carefully squeezed the glue onto the wound to finish the job.

"Done. Don't move yet. I want to make sure the glue dries before I turn you over and see what else I need to fix." Abby was a beautiful woman, especially sprawled on the floor, looking so vulnerable. Her dark brown hair had that sexy tousled appearance that women sometimes had after a night of making love with someone. Not that she'd ever experienced that firsthand, but this was a fact that romance writers often described in their books. Even through her confused expression, Abby's vivid blue eyes were a vision of loveliness. They sparkled in the bright bath lighting.

"I've been in a more comfortable position when a woman was leaning over me while on my back. Can I move yet?"

Muse was amused. Something about this woman tickled her funny bone, and she chuckled. She placed her hand under

Abby's back and helped her to sit. "Okay, blatant flirting aside, let me examine the back of your head." Muse carefully palpated Abby's head.

"Ouch, yeah there. That's a little tender."

"Mmhm. Big goose egg, but I don't feel any stickiness. Do you have any other sore spots I can check out?"

"I think I broke my ass."

Muse raised her eyebrow.

"Honestly, that was not a line just to get you to stroke my butt." Abby shifted to her side and began rubbing her bottom. "It wouldn't be the first time I've broken my tailbone. Trust me, it isn't pleasant. I won't be able to sit for six weeks."

"Shall I make you an ice pack?" Muse asked.

"Nah, I'll go find my donut."

"I don't think stress eating is going to help with the swelling."

Abby erupted into a fit of laughter. "While a chocolate donut does sound divine right about now, I was referring to an orthopedic seat cushion in the shape of a donut."

Muse blushed. "Oh, right, that makes sense." Standing, Muse offered her hand.

Abby took hold and let Muse pull her to a standing position. "Thanks."

Muse moved in close to inspect the super glued wound, and Abby's eyes went wide. She was nodding when Abby coughed uncomfortably. "I think I did a pretty good job. You shouldn't have a noticeable scar."

"Oh, uh, I thought you were going to…"

Muse wrinkled her nose. "Going to what?"

"Never mind. It was partially wishful thinking, but more astonishment, I suppose."

"You're an odd one." Muse smiled to soften what might be considered a negative assessment.

"So I've been told. Like a thousand times." Abby grinned in response.

"Surely, that's hyperbole."

"You don't understand sarcasm, do you?" Abby chuckled as she began to walk stiffly into the other room.

Muse opened her mouth and began nodding. "Oh, that was sarcasm. Got it."

Abby patted Muse's shoulder. "And they call me odd." Abby pivoted. "Before I forget or Goddess forbid, fall again, I'd like to get warmer clothes for you." Abby pointed to Muse's cover-up. "That is entirely too distracting, and if we decide to take another walk on the beach later, you'll appreciate my sweats. Unless you'd rather go back to your place and change."

"I would appreciate borrowing some clothes. I haven't quite secured accommodations yet. I had my eye on the Kalaloch cabins. They seem very cozy and close enough to the beach to satisfy my vision of an appropriate vacation."

"Obviously, since I'm a local, I've never stayed in one. Never even looked at the inside, so I'll take your word for it. The restaurant, on the other hand, is practically my second home. Best food for miles. Well…the only food that I don't cook for myself, for miles. We should go there for dinner," Abby added as an apparent afterthought. "There is a pizza place, but that's farther down the road and…" Abby's voice trailed off.

"I'd like that."

"Wait, so where are your clothes and things if you haven't secured lodgings yet?"

Muse shrugged. "I thought I could worry about that later. The beach was calling to me."

"Where are you from again? I don't think you ever revealed that little tidbit. Why do you seem familiar, although I'm sure I would remember if we'd ever met before?"

Muse adeptly changed the subject. "I am chilled, the sweats?"

"Oh, right, right. Coming up." Abby hurried away, deftly avoiding the coffee table this time.

CHAPTER THREE

Abby wasn't fooled by Muse's attempt to distract her from what she considered a relatively innocuous question. Where a person was from fit squarely into the *small talk* category. Abby had met her fair share of homeless people who had gone from middle-class to homeless in less time than it took a Tesla to go from zero to sixty. The reasons were varied. Sometimes it was mental health issues left unchecked and untreated. Other times it was the loss of a job and no safety net to fall back on.

For now, she would play Muse's game. Abby was a sucker for a hard-luck story. Poking her head out of the bedroom, she called out, "Why don't you stay with me. I have plenty of room, and I could be your personal tour guide." Tossing her offer out like a feather catching a gust of wind, she waited to see where it would land.

"Really? You're not just making the offer because you're an exceptionally nice person…"

"No, I'd love the company, especially since my writer's block has taken root and is growing exponentially like overgrown blackberry bushes. Have you ever tried to remove blackberry bushes that remain unchecked? Those roots are like the badasses of bushes." Abby walked out of her bedroom, holding a warm sweatshirt, T-shirt, sweatpants, and socks.

"Thank you. I accept. You're one of the primary artists I wanted to get to know a bit more. I'm truly sorry about your block. I'm more than a little responsible for that." Muse held her hands out and accepted the clothing.

Abby rubbed her eyebrow. "Don't be ridiculous. I hear that writer's block happens to the best authors. Why should I escape that fate? Lately, I haven't had a hit. Readers want romance or romantic intrigue, and I'm bored with that. I've gone outside the rails. That probably has more to do with the block than anything else."

"If it makes you feel any better, I've had substandard evaluations on my job performance for the last year. Thus, the vacation. I may not even have a job to return to. And, that's a bit scary for me because I wouldn't know what to expect."

Bingo. She lost her job and was either too proud to admit it or still in shock. "Um, you can change in the bedroom or bathroom—your choice. I didn't grab a bra or underwear. I suppose you can either continue to wear your swimsuit underneath or go commando. Personally, I rarely wear undergarments. I don't have the kind of job that requires me to dress up. This" —Abby waved her hand over her body— "is as good as it gets. I'll throw on a pair of jeans and a nice shirt on occasion, but that's about as far as I'll go."

"Sweats look good on you." Muse's eyes journeyed over Abby's body, lazily taking in her appearance. It was unsettling and yet, mildly arousing.

"Oh, now you're just bald-faced lying to me. But who am I to push away a compliment, even if it isn't truthful?"

"I never lie. I may avoid telling the whole story. For very good reasons, I might add, but I would never tell an untruth. It's against the rules."

"What rules?" As if her curiosity were a thermometer, it rose another degree. Surely, Abby was on her way to boiling. Was this only curiosity or something more?

"The rules I live by and the ones he gave me." The statement was delivered with a fair amount of nonchalance. Muse maintained direct eye contact, seemingly challenging Abby to simply accept her explanation at face value.

"By whom?" Abby continued her questioning as she moved a few inches closer to Muse. She was going to get to the bottom of this mystery.

"Can I change now so that we may take another walk and perhaps have dinner? I am starting to experience hunger. It's not a pleasant feeling."

Another redirection. "I can relate. I get quite hangry when I don't feed the beast."

Muse chuckled. "I like that made-up word—hangry. I first read that in a book. She was a colleague's inspired author. I wanted to expand my horizons and went outside of my territory to read that one."

Editor? Maybe Muse is an unemployed editor? Abby wondered if Muse had priced herself outside the market with the explosion of Kindle Unlimited and the need to find cheaper editors who would do the work. Could Muse be an editor of Lesfic? While Abby was contemplating her latest theory on Muse, she had walked into the bathroom and closed the door.

***

Abby's clothes fit reasonably well. Although Muse was a bit taller than Abby, she surmised that Abby tended to buy her clothes a size larger than necessary for comfort.

Muse needed to tread carefully. Abby kept asking questions that she could not answer if she wanted to be truthful. So far, Muse was able to avoid her curiosity. Muse wondered if she allowed a person to come to their own conclusions, and those assessments were inaccurate, would she be telling lies by not correcting the speculation?

"Are we able to go to this restaurant you speak of in these clothes?" Muse asked.

Abby's brow wrinkled. "We can, I suppose. I don't believe they have a dress code. Although Kalaloch Lodge is one of those places I tend to visit dressed in jeans and a nice shirt. Maybe we should go to your car to get your suitcase."

"I don't have a suitcase. Or a car. I was planning on securing transportation after my stroll on the beach."

"Um, okay. Do you somehow have a wad of cash stuffed in your swimsuit? I've heard of padding one's bra, but this would certainly be a novel way to do that." The wolfish smile returned.

"Oh, dear, I did not plan this well." Muse frowned at her insistence on jumping into her vacation on a whim. In the past, rash decisions had always led to trouble.

"Forget about it. Let's go in what we're wearing. It'll be fine, I promise."

Muse didn't like how Abby's gaze dropped to her feet, and she wouldn't look her in the eyes. "You pity me," Muse stated. She took a step back as she gazed upon Abby wide-eyed.

"Oh, Goddess, no. Um…I…shit…damn, for a writer, I can't find the right words. I always offend you. I don't know how I manage to so successfully screw things up."

Muse did not want Abby to pity her, but she liked this self-flagellation even less. Extending her hand to Abby's shoulder, she awkwardly patted her. "Come on, let's go slumming. That's what you call it, right? I'll trust your judgment that our attire doesn't matter as long as we have the money to pay."

"In this neck of the woods, that's very true. I should have gone there in my sweats before. Breaking that self-inflicted barrier will be freeing. I can't explain how comfortable I feel in sweats. Daytime pajamas are my favorite way of dressing. I practically live in them already, so I might as well take the next step. As long as you don't mind being seen with me in my comfy clothes?"

Muse smiled. "Not at all. As I said before, you're quite fetching in your warm covering with a hood. I am eager to experience so many new things. Wearing daytime pajamas to a restaurant seems a good place to start."

***

The short trek to the beach along the well-worn path only took a few minutes. Abby forgot to ask Muse about the long trek to the restaurant. She was so used to walking everywhere, she hadn't given it a second thought until she looked at Muse's feet and noticed the flip flops. In Abby's humble opinion, that footwear was not the most comfortable when attempting long distances. She hadn't noticed that Muse had not put on the socks she'd been given earlier.

"The walk on the beach is a few miles. I forgot to check if that was okay with you. We can turn around and take my car if you'd prefer."

"No, no, I want to walk on the beach. May I take your hand? I've read about this in books. It's supposed to be very romantic."

Abby coughed. "Um, yes. Have you never held a woman's hand? Are you uh…struggling with your uh…"

Muse's light tickle of laughter floated in the air and blended with the sounds of the seagulls. "I'm not experiencing the kind of struggle you're referring to. I haven't held a woman's hand before, but not for the reasons you presume. I've made you uncomfortable. That was not my intent."

Screw it. Abby was not going to turn down the opportunity to hold this beautiful woman's hand. She held out her arm and intertwined their fingers when Muse's soft skin touched her own. "You'll be okay to walk that far in your flip flops?"

Muse frowned. "I believe so. Are these not the correct footwear to walk the beach?"

Abby shrugged. "I suppose for some, but not for me." Abby felt giddy with emotion as their arms swung together as if they were two young girls playing innocently on the beach.

"I would like to ask a question." Muse paused before quickly continuing. "Your vision of love is so beautiful in your books. Is it based on personal experiences? I've heard that authors must write what they know."

Abby laughed. "Hardly, or there would be a lot of psychopathic lesbian serial killers out there." She shuddered.

"Have you never been in love?" The intensity of Muse's look hit her square in the gut. She was not prepared for how intrusive this question suddenly felt to her.

"I thought I was in love once, but it turns out it was a prolonged case of indigestion. To add insult to injury, the other person did not suffer along with me." Abby grinned.

"That's funny. You should use that line in one of your books."

"It's not that funny. I'm not that funny. It wasn't intended as a joke. Shit comes out of my mouth before I have a chance to screen my words." Abby's body relaxed as their conversation turned away from the topic of her nonexistent love life. The recent heartbreak was still too raw.

"Your readers think you're funny."

"I guess some of them do. I was asked once to be on a humor panel. In the privacy of my own home, I looked around, even though the request came through an email. I thought they were joking. Turns out, they weren't. I called myself the accidental humorist for weeks. I joked about that in my weekly blog. Poking fun at myself is my favorite pastime."

"Um, yes, I've noticed."

Abby stopped walking and placed her free hand above her brow, squinting into the sunshine as she turned to face Muse. "Please tell me you aren't a rabid fan who's going to tie me to my bed…wait…what am I saying…go for it…that might be fun."

"See, funny. I would not classify myself as what you might call a rabid fan, but I'm familiar with your writings. I suppose I could claim that I'm intimately familiar."

"Intimately familiar. I like that. Unless that's a nice way of stating you're a crazy reader who follows my every word on whatever social media site I inconsistently frequent. Muse, you're an interesting present that I look forward to unwrapping. Unfortunately, you appear to have an inordinate amount of tape keeping the beautiful wrapping in place."

"Do you think we can watch the sunset sitting against a log tonight? I would like to do that, too."

"Uh," Abby hedged. "Sunset occurs kinda late here in the Northwest, especially at the beginning of summer."

"Oh." Muse's shoulders drooped.

The disappointment in Muse's voice affected Abby more than she wanted it to. "We should take our time with dinner, have several drinks, and get silly drunk. Then it will take us longer than normal to walk back. I believe that would result in the perfect timing to catch the sunset."

"Thank you, Abby."

"You're welcome." Abby squeezed Muse's hand.

CHAPTER FOUR

Muse giggled again as she swayed down the weathered wood steps of the restaurant. The euphoric feeling was new to her. The beverages they'd ordered were having an unusual effect. She'd always avoided the free-flowing wine whenever Dionysus made an appearance.

She'd watched as Abby squirmed on the hard chair, readjusting the inflatable donut several times before finding the right spot. With each new drink, Abby seemed to relax, and Muse wondered if the alcohol was helping with her discomfort.

"Is your tailbone feeling better?" Muse asked as she carefully navigated the final step.

"Yup, but I don't think it has anything to do with this stupid donut that I tossed in my pack. Alcohol provides multiple side benefits, all rolled into a tasty treat."

"I never thought mixing salty, sweet, and sour would taste so good," Muse enthused.

"I know, right? Those Sweet and Sour Cherry Salty Dogs went down far too easily. I probably should have stopped at two. You definitely should have stopped at two." Abby put her hand on her mouth and snickered.

"Is this how you have managed to fall all the time? Is it alcohol-related?"

"Oh, no. Ironically, I'm more careful when I'm tipsy." Abby wrinkled her nose. "I think you're on to something. I should drink more. It's better for my overall health." She giggled to punctuate her revelation.

Muse stumbled on an uneven step and landed on her knee. "I don't believe alcohol is as good for me."

Abby rushed to Muse's side and helped her stand. "Are you okay? Goddess, I'm sorry, I should not have plied you with all that alcohol. You probably think I have nefarious motives and plan on taking advantage of you when we return to my place."

"I'm fine. Can we still watch the sunset?"

"Uh-huh. It's getting chilly, so we should go back to my house, get a blanket, and then walk to the beach. We'll have plenty of time, even if we wobble all the way." Abby giggled again.

Muse's brain was fuzzy and having a hard time paying attention to her words. She retook Abby's hand because the sensation earlier was so pleasant. She wanted to feel the connection again. Abby didn't seem to mind.

"Your hand is so small," Muse noted.

"Yeah, good thing small hands on women don't equate to other small appendages that are important…"

"You're making fun of the myth that the size of a man's penis is dependent on the size of his hands? Why would a lesbian bother with such things?" Muse asked.

Abby shrugged. "I am curious about a lot of things. I looked up this myth once."

"Of course you did." Muse's smile revealed the mirth behind her statement. "You're about to educate me, aren't you?"

"Yes, yes, I am. Apparently, there is a tiny correlation between the length of a man's ring finger compared to his index finger and the size of his penis. Not only that, but if their ring finger is longer, they appear more attractive, have more sex partners, are more athletic, and are more attentive to women. Oh, and women also have more sex partners if their ring finger is longer."

"Why does the size matter? Would a lesbian want a larger dildo to experience satisfaction?"

Abby pushed her hand through her hair. "Um…I suppose it might matter to some. I guess it's important for women who prefer vaginal versus clitoral orgasms." Abby rubbed her hand over her face before continuing. "Goddess, I sound like a sex therapist. I only know this stuff because I do a lot of research for my books. I don't have that much experience with…"

"Sex?"

"Uh…yeah. I'd like to ask you a personal question because I feel like you're sending mixed messages."

"Of course. I'll answer honestly if I can."

"Are you a lesbian?"

Muse tilted her head to the side. This was an unexpected question. "I don't know."

"Oh." The disappointment dripped from Abby's response like a leaky roof.

"I've never had to consider that before. I'm sorry I don't have an answer."

"Haven't you ever been in a relationship or been in love?" Abby asked.

"No, that's why I wish to experience romance and love—separately from the pages of a book. I'm most intrigued by how you've described this in your novels. I figured you would be the best person to help."

"So, is this a date or something?" Abby tugged at the bottom of her hoodie with her free hand.

"Let's call it 'or something' for now. Although, I am intrigued by the concept of dating, which seems to have evolved over the ages. It's different today than say back in the 900s, the 1400s, or 1900s."

"Wow! You must be extremely well-read. I didn't even know there were romances set back that far. Which era do you prefer?"

"That's an excellent question. I don't know. They all have their pros and cons." With each step, Muse felt the giddy effect of the alcohol subside. The two women started to delve into more serious topics of discussion that Muse was not prepared to respond to. Abby tried to ask her about her family, but how could she possibly answer those questions? It wasn't like family was a trigger, exactly. Maybe it was the mere notion of the absence of a traditional family that caused the discomfort. Regardless, getting too personal with Abby was strictly taboo. Her boss' warnings surfaced.

***

Zeus, Musetta's boss, sat regally on an ornately carved stone chair. The man was imposing enough with his imperial presence, and Musetta didn't believe he needed the pomp and circumstance of the room to add to her anxiety. A bowl of fruit and something else she wasn't sure about sat atop a hunk of polished marble. The swirling patterns in the finely crafted table distracted her.

She'd been summoned, and this was the place Zeus always chose to have crucial conversations. *No wonder his posture is so rigid, sitting on that uncomfortable hunk of rock despite how beautifully designed it was.* She recognized the style and smiled, knowing she'd played a small part in the brilliance of the carving.

"Will you call yourself Musetta?" he asked.

"Yes, that's my name. Plus, it means little muse. I quite like it."

"Hmm, that's an unusual name for down there. Aren't you afraid you'll stick out too much?" Zeus rubbed his chin. "For the record, I don't like this plan of yours, but I suppose we have no option. You have not performed to your potential for some time now. You may have three days. That's all we can afford without our subjects beginning to ask questions and wonder what is happening."

"I know, I know. Death was given three days, and those consequences were more devastating than my vacation will ever cause."

"Don't be so sure about that." Zeus looked away, and Muse got the feeling he was hiding something big.

"Anything else I should know?" Muse asked her boss.

"The rules for your excursion are simple. Don't reveal yourself unless necessary, but don't lie. If you must be truthful, to avoid a lie, be sure to limit that to only one person. You must blend in. In other words, don't do anything that will cause too much exposure. Finally, you must avoid getting involved with one of your subjects."

"Involved? How can I possibly avoid that? The whole purpose of my holiday is to seek answers so that I may perform, as you said before, to my potential," she huffed.

"Very well, you may connect with one of your subjects, but don't take it too far. Finally, if you break any of these rules, I can't have you back. Your services will no longer be needed, and you will forfeit your immortality. Those are the minimum consequences. You may face other penalties for your disobedience depending on my mood."

"How am I supposed to blend in? Will I be able to obtain resources like money to purchase the necessary trinkets and attire?"

He waved his hand in the air. "Yes, yes. Simply concentrate on your need, and it will appear."

"Cool." She grinned, hoping she did not look like an adolescent who'd just received permission to take the car.

"Pfft," he scoffed. "You're already talking like one of them. I suppose that will assist you in blending in. Have you decided where you will visit?"

"Yes, I would like to go to that beach near Forks, Washington."

"Ah, the place where Abigail Prentice lives." Zeus nodded as if he knew something she didn't.

"Yes, I've been failing her more than any of the others. I want to understand why. She used to be one of my most successful subjects."

"I must admit, I applaud your desire to go right to the root of your failing."

"Root of my failing? Do you believe this Abigail is the key?"

"Perhaps. Yes, I believe that is so." Zeus nodded his head, confirming his theory. "You've focused on her more than the others for quite some time now. You've been quite enamored with her writings. That, more than anything else, is out of the norm for us. We don't focus on any one person. I might even call it an obsession. I hope history is not repeating itself. At least it won't result in another…"

"History? What are you talking about? Calli had that same pinched look when I asked her about this. You two are keeping something from me." Muse narrowed her eyes.

"Never mind that. You don't get to interrogate me. I'm allowing this against my better judgment. Would you rather I cancel this three-day vacation?"

"No, please don't. I'm sorry. Anything else?" Muse asked.

"Don't become too enmeshed in their world. Artists have a way of sucking us in. Temptation is not something we're immune to."

"Isn't that the point? I want to be sucked in. Only then can I truly understand what has been happening to me." She grinned in excitement.

"Exercise caution. That's an order."

"Very well. Can I go now?" Muse crossed her arms in petulance. *Why am I acting like a human teenager?*

He waved her away, and she found herself standing on the beach, looking at the small waves crashing gently against the sandy shoreline. The sun was shining as she looked to the sky, but a slight shiver traveled through her body. She looked at her sheer swimsuit cover and was about to concentrate on a need for warmer clothing when she noticed an attractive woman fall face-first into the sand, no more than ten yards in front of her.

***

Abby looked at Muse and saw several emotions flash across her face before she adopted a blank expression. Abby thought she recognized apprehension, confusion, and maybe a tiny amount of fear. She got the sense Muse had gone somewhere. She'd seen people do that before. She'd probably done that herself—taken a short mental journey while remembering something. It didn't necessarily have to be anything unpleasant. Abby wanted to know about Muse's journey.

"Where'd you go just now?"

Muse shook her head. "I was recalling a conversation with my boss. It's not important." Suddenly, Muse turned and grabbed her arm. Continuing to hold on, she exclaimed, "Let's go on a long motorcycle ride tomorrow."

"You have a motorcycle?"

"I will tomorrow."

"Cryptic again." Abby sighed. "Where is this beast? Should we go and get it along with your bags, which I assume are attached."

"Tomorrow will be soon enough. Come on." Muse tugged Abby's sleeve and pulled her along. "We have to hurry. The sun is almost to the horizon. We still need to get your blanket and return to the beach."

"Okay." Abby chuckled. "I'm coming. Well, not literally," she mumbled.

"What?"

"Never mind. It was a crass afterthought that I would prefer you to ignore."

"All right," Muse answered cheerily. There was a bounce in her step as they made their way on the path from the beach to her house.

"Um, Muse, I hope the sunset tonight won't disappoint you too much. Whenever there aren't many clouds, the sunsets are quite boring."

"Not to me. First encounters are never boring. Events are only boring after you've experienced them too many times to count. I suppose that's why falling in love is so thrilling at first, because it's new and exciting. I wonder, are there adventures that never get old?"

"I'd like to think waking next to the woman you love—every single day—would never get old. I would cherish that. Or I'd like to think I would."

"What a lovely thing to say. I don't understand why you're single. You have an attractive face and body. You write beautiful stories. You have kindness in your heart. What is the problem? What fault do you possess?" The earnestness of Muse's questions did not hold a hint of malice.

Abby clutched her sweatshirt, where her heart was located. "Ouch. Go right to it. I don't know. I've never found the one, I guess. Plus, writers aren't the easiest people to live with. Romance writers generally have inflated notions of love. I suppose our expectations of the perfect partner are extremely high because we match them against the characters that we draw on our pages."

"You write flawed characters, surely those in real life could match up."

"I live in my sweats and in my head. Conversation is sometimes awkward and limited. I'm not a very fun person to be around. Dates are usually a disaster. Getting to a second date is damn near impossible for me."

"We've had some lovely conversations. And, I've learned about penis size. You have a plethora of information to share with others."

Abby cringed. "I don't think my odd research appeals to many lesbians. Case in point, how I relayed my research on penis size to you. Good thing you're an odd duck yourself." Abby slapped her hand across her mouth. "Oh, Goddess," she groaned, "that did not come out correctly."

Muse chuckled. "I am odd, and there is nothing wrong with that. Own it. Your oddness, that is."

"What size shoe do you wear?" Abby pointed at Muse's feet.

Muse stopped in front of the house and crinkled her brow. "I don't know."

"Okay…I'll just run in the house and get a blanket. Then I'll grab socks and my sturdy slippers that can pass as a pair of slip-on shoes. They'll be better than those flip flops. Hopefully, they'll fit." Abby scrutinized Muse's feet. "Yeah, they might work."

***

The large piece of driftwood nearly a hundred yards beyond the edge of the path provided the perfect place for Abby and Muse to sit and watch the sunset. By the time the sun dipped low onto the horizon, a few more clouds had rolled in. What Abby feared might turn into a two-color sunset with some minor variance ended up creating the perfect explosion of color for the ultimate visual experience. The joyful yellow evolved into a fiery striation of orange and red against the bright blue background. Warm and cold hues crashed together in a kind of passionate dance that Abby knew happened every single night, nonetheless it was still breathtaking when seen through Muse's eyes.

"How could anyone ever take this for granted? It's like Monet painted this sky just for us," Muse gushed.

Abby sighed and let her head fall on Muse's shoulder. As if by instinct, Muse draped her arm around Abby and pulled her close. Sitting slightly on her side, using one butt cheek, was the only comfortable position for Abby as they watched the sun descend on the horizon. For a while, she could ignore her injured tailbone. The two women stayed seated together for several minutes as the complete cycle ended and the stars began to appear, along with the bright light of a full moon reflecting off the water.

Muse turned her head to face Abby, and their lips were mere inches apart. "Thank you for sharing this with me," she whispered.

It would have been so easy to close the distance. Abby didn't believe Muse would have rejected her, but for whatever reason, those last few inches seemed too wide a gulf to cross. Abby didn't know if Muse was a lesbian. She wasn't interested in a toaster oven. Being someone's first was not a role Abby was eager to play. She was awkward enough around women who were 100% lesbian. Besides, the recent disaster with Jenny was still fresh in her mind.

Abby cleared her throat. "Um, yeah, of course. We should head back. It's late now. I need to make up the guest room. Besides, I keep shifting my position to relieve pressure on my tailbone, and that has to mar the experience for you."

"Do I make you nervous?" Muse asked.

"A little, yes."

"Why?"

"Um, I'm a lesbian through and through, and you are, without a doubt, the most beautiful woman I've ever met. Confession…"

"Yes?"

"When I met you, the first thought that came to mind was that you must be Helen of Troy come to life."

Muse threw back her head and laughed. She stood and offered her hand to Abby. "If we retire for the evening, can we please get up early? I want to squeeze as much as I can into this vacation. I only have two full days left."

"What kind of vacation is that where they only give you three days off? That's not a vacation. That's a long weekend."

"Mmm, maybe, but it's what I was allowed." Muse looked to the ocean. "I hope it's enough time."

Abby shared that dream. The news that she only had two more days with Muse was like a bucket of cold water on a blistering hot day. Shocking reality. She hoped that in that small time frame, she might learn more about Muse. *Perhaps she lives close by.* Wishful thinking on her part, but Abby did not have the heart to consider another alternative. Muse had come into her life for a reason. She was sure of it.

CHAPTER FIVE

Something strangely wonderful reached Muse's nose. She stretched her body and breathed in deeply, hoping to capture more of this magnificent smell. When she'd gotten close to the restaurant, a similar sensation had occurred. Abby had explained it was the blending of garlic and other spices.

"When the chef applies heat to the various combinations, the aroma wafts through the air attracting unsuspecting tourists." Abby had smiled and didn't look away for several seconds. "Taste and smell work together. It's like that with romance, too."

"I think I would like to taste romance. That sounds almost as good as this meal." Muse had answered.

The smell had been a potent precursor to the flavor of their meal. Each morsel burst with delight on her tongue. She looked forward to her next meal, hoping she might experience other glorious flavors.

This new smell was so different from the others, yet just as powerful. Jumping from the bed, Muse rushed toward the aroma, following her nose to the kitchen. A flash of orange fur dashed in front of her, making a beeline to Abby's bedroom. She presumed that it was Plato and almost followed to get a better look, but the incredible smell was far too distracting. Muse hoped that at some point, she could make friends with Abby's pet. She'd never had that experience before and desperately wanted to run her hands along his body. Perhaps she would hear the rumble in his throat.

Abby was standing in front of the refrigerator, staring at the contents inside. She jumped when Muse came close.

"Oh, you're up. I was trying to figure out what to cook for breakfast. I have eggs and turkey bacon. I can pull bread from the freezer. I made coffee, but maybe you'd prefer tea. I didn't know. I can put the teakettle back on," Abby rambled.

"Is that wonderful smell coffee?"

Abby turned to face Muse with a crinkled brow. "Probably."

"Then I will have coffee."

"I don't much like the taste myself, so I add lots of creamer. How do you like your coffee?" Abby pulled a carton of eggs from the refrigerator and set them on the counter.

"I'll take it the same as you. I trust your judgment. Your suggestions last night were perfect. Can I help?"

Abby pointed to the small dinette. "Nah, go sit down, and I'll bring you coffee." She opened the refrigerator and hesitated. "You know what, I think I'll make scrambled eggs with smoked salmon instead of turkey bacon. Yeah, that would be good," she mumbled as she retrieved butter, milk, and the smoked salmon. Juggling the items in her hands, she bumped the refrigerator door closed with her hip.

Muse thought Abby looked cute with her oversized T-shirt and pajama bottoms that dragged across the floor. The bright yellow smiley faces matched Muse's mood. She wished she had a pair instead of the sweats she'd worn to bed. "I like your pajamas."

Abby turned her head and blushed. "Oh, um, these were a gift from my brother. He hoped they would help me get over my block. They arrived in the mail the other day. I thought they couldn't hurt, and I've been wearing them ever since."

"Is this writer's block such a terrible thing?"

Abby did a kind of half-shrug, half-tilt of her head. "I suppose there are worse things to happen to a person, even if they make their living as a writer. The biggest problem I have is not obsessing over the fact that I haven't written a single word in several months." Abby pulled a bowl from her cabinet and began cracking eggs. "I don't own a TV, so eventually, I'll run out of programs to binge-watch on the subscription services I've allowed myself. Right now, they are my only form of entertainment. Oh, and social media sucks my time as well. At least I have other authors to commiserate with. Although none have experienced the same level of writer's block that I have."

Muse followed her nose and found the dark black liquid in the glass container sitting on the counter. "This is the coffee, right?" Muse found an empty cup and poured the steaming drink inside.

"Oh, yes, I'm sorry." Abby swiveled to the sink, washed her hands, then retrieved a large container of creamer from the refrigerator. She began to pour the thick liquid into the cup and looked at Muse, pausing before asking, "How much cream would you like?"

"However much you normally use."

Abby tipped the jug and topped off Muse's coffee. "Go on, sit down and relax. Breakfast won't take long."

"I would like to get my motorcycle and bring it to your house after breakfast. Would that be okay?"

"You really have a motorcycle? Wow! I can't wait to take a ride with you. I haven't been on the back of a motorcycle in years. I love them." Abby vibrated with energy.

"I'll have one, yes."

"Huh?" The line in Abby's forehead deepened in confusion.

Muse almost slapped herself for revealing that she had not yet procured the transportation item that seemed to delight Abby. Changing the topic always appeared to work. Although Muse knew this would not continue forever.

"Are you sure I can't assist? I believe I could handle stirring the eggs." Muse sipped her coffee. "Mmm, this is good. I like this coffee."

"It's the caramel flavoring. If you really want to help, maybe you can make the toast." Abby opened the freezer and grabbed a loaf of bread. She tossed it on the counter and pointed to a silver toaster. "I just want one piece."

Muse peered at the two slots and nodded to herself as she untwisted the fastener on the bread. All the slices of bread were uniform, and Muse wondered how they managed to accomplish this. She placed two pieces inside the toaster, hesitating before pushing on the lever and then smiling to herself when she saw the wires inside the slots turn red. "Ingenious," she muttered.

"The butter is on the counter. Don't put too much on mine. I prefer slathering my toast with jam." Abby pulled a knife from the drawer and handed it to Muse.

Muse continued to stare at the toaster. When the bread popped, she jumped back, startled by the sudden ejection. A small plate sat next to the toaster. Finding the toast hot to the touch, Muse quickly released the pieces onto the plate. She watched in wonder when the slices of butter began to melt, and she spread what was quickly turning to liquid evenly over the squares.

Abby kept turning around to look at Muse while whisking the eggs in the bowl. She chuckled when she caught Muse buttering the bread. "You act like this is brand new to you. Your child-like innocence is very hard to resist."

"I've read it's the small things in life we ought to embrace and cherish." No matter how much she had read, there were new experiences to discover. She sighed. Three days wouldn't be enough, but it was all she had.

"Muse, I believe you'll be a terrific influence on me."

***

Abby hadn't opened her laptop or peeked at her iPad in nearly twenty-four hours. She was itching to see what she was missing. Her only means of learning what was happening in the world was through social media and her news apps. After clearing the dishes and cleaning up, she had asked if Muse wanted Abby to go with her to get her motorcycle. Muse had answered quickly, almost too quickly, that she didn't need any help. The response was odd, but Abby desperately wanted to access her tablet, so she didn't give it a second thought.

Hurrying to her bedroom, she grabbed her iPad and opened her news app only to find same old same old. Multiple dings in rapid succession caught her eye. Right now, there was a hot thread happening in one of her favorite writers' groups. She read the latest post.

I swear, I literally lost my ability to complete the sentence I was writing yesterday. It was like my mind went blank.

Ding. A new post appeared. *OMG, the same thing happened to me. This is like a new form of writer's block. I was flowing, and then all of a sudden, nothing. Like a switch flipped off. This kind of abruptness has never happened to me.*

Not even bothering to sit, Abby began a quick scan through a slew of similar posts and tried to make sense of what she was reading. Interspersed between the posts from writers lamenting about not writing were the typical supportive posts from authors who weren't having any difficulties. Familiar words like, *be kind to yourself,* or *you deserve a break.*

An unusual pattern began to emerge as she kept reading. All the authors who were experiencing a block lived in the Pacific Northwest, and most of the authors sending notations of support lived in other parts of the world. Odd.

As Abby prepared to respond with her own post, she heard the squeak of the front door and looked up. Muse was smiling, her cheeks flushed. She carried a saddlebag in her hand. *Ok, so maybe Muse isn't homeless after all,* Abby thought. Muse was such an enigma to Abby, and she was desperate to learn more. Abby was still glad she'd invited Muse to stay with her. She was racking her brain to get the tight-lipped woman to reveal more. In the meantime, having a beautiful woman fill in the empty spaces in your life wasn't the worst thing that could happen to her while she was waiting for inspiration to return.

"Hey you. I see you brought your clothes." Flipping her tablet over to keep from any distraction that would pull her back, Abby leaned against the wall and picked up her second cup of coffee. "I need to take a shower and probably put on sturdy jeans. I'm not sure if my propensity for falling and injuring myself extends to possible motorcycle accidents. I figure I better wear something to protect me from road rash."

"I'll choose jeans as well. I do not want a rash from the road. It can't be that hard, driving a motorcycle, can it?"

Abby's jaw hung open before she squeaked, "Please tell me you're joking. You have a license to operate a motorcycle, right?"

"Um. Well, I did not realize that was required."

Abby bowed her head and poked her forehead in a gesture of exasperation. "Wait. You're pulling my leg." She smacked her head. "I'm such an idiot. Of course, you know how to drive a motorcycle. That's how you got here? Where are you from again?"

"Oh, not too far." Muse pointed to the tablet. "May I look at your device while you shower?"

"Sure. Knock yourself out."

Abby chuckled as she carried her coffee into the bedroom and began pulling clothes from her dresser to take into the bathroom. She hoped her tailbone injury would be less painful on a motorcycle than in a car. At least she'd be able to lean forward, and that would relieve the pressure on her sore behind. The vibration might not help, but she could worry about that later. She was not about to give up a chance to feel the freedom of riding on a motorcycle again.

***

Muse had read about YouTube and quickly sent a silent thanks to the universe when she found the tiny red box with the white arrow. After several tries, she touched the small magnifying glass picture and typed, *how to drive a motorcycle.* The young man on the video started with clothing recommendations, and Muse was glad he had provided such useful information. She made minor adjustments to what she'd added to her saddlebag.

Halfway through the video, Muse wondered why she'd had the bright idea of a motorcycle versus a car. Right about now, a car seemed far less complicated. She also worried about Abby and how this might affect her tailbone. Her face was mere inches from the screen as she concentrated on his instructions.

A few minutes after Muse heard the water in the shower end, the bathroom door opened. Abby's head appeared, and she asked, "What are you doing?"

Muse poked at the screens looking for a way to stop the video. Finally, she hit the perpendicular equal sign. Muse didn't have time to wonder how an equal sign was the answer to stopping the darn thing and saving her from embarrassment. She looked up and smiled.

"Nothing. Just checking this out. Convenient device. I like it."

"Okaay. Um, listen, I still have to dry my hair. Are you going to be alright out there? Shit, I should have offered the shower to you first. I'll take my dryer with me, and you can hop in the shower now."

"I can wait. It's fine."

Abby ducked back into the bathroom, and Muse breathed a sigh of relief. She'd managed to view most of the video and decided it might be prudent to attempt a short practice run while Abby finished with her hair.

After she'd snuck outside, she straddled the motorcycle and started the engine like the video had demonstrated. She made sure the bike was in neutral because the young man had emphasized how important that was.

Squeezing the left lever, she recited, "Clutch, check." The right brake was stiff, but she nodded and exclaimed, "Brake, check."

Exhilaration flooded her body when she rolled the throttle. The loud rumble was the coolest thing she'd ever heard. She felt invincible. She was ready to give it a go. Gripping the clutch, Muse depressed the lever near her right foot to put the bike in gear one. She remembered the man warning her not to let the clutch out too quickly because it would cause the bike to cut out. Muse was more worried about giving the throttle too much gas and popping a wheelie or losing control.

She lurched forward, and the jerky movement of the bike almost caused her to lose it as she rolled down the driveway. If her hands hadn't been occupied at the moment, she would have patted herself on the back. This was going to be fun.

Concentrating so intently on her practice run, Muse almost missed Abby standing in the open door with a puzzled expression on her face. Confusion set in, and she grabbed the brake instead of the clutch. The darn thing jerked to a stop, toppling over in the process.

Abby began running until she reached Muse and the motorcycle that had fallen painfully on top of Muse. She grabbed the handlebars helping to pull the steel monstrosity upright. "Holy shit. Are you all right?"

A sheepish smile appeared on Muse's face. "You distracted me. That outfit is very fetching. I like your black boots. They will go well with the motorcycle."

"Please tell me this is your motorcycle. Oh, my Goddess. You stole a bike from a tourist, and the police are going to come looking for you. I'll be labeled a co-conspirator." Abby's voice began to escalate to a high-pitched rant as she spiraled out of control. "They'll throw us both in prison, but we'll be separated at first, just like in *Orange is the New Black*. I look terrible in orange. In fact, nobody looks good in that color, except maybe people who are considered *Falls* in that stupid color draping. But you and I are definitely not *Falls*."

Muse put the kickstand down and quickly reached Abby, placing a calming hand on her shoulder. "Abby, stop. I did not steal this motorcycle. I'll admit that I'm a bit rusty. I was doing a practice run."

"How did you get the bike here?"

Rubbing the side of her leg, she winced. "I walked it." Technically, she had walked the bike to the start of Abby's driveway, so this wasn't a lie.

"From where? You did hurt yourself. I should take a look."

"Not far from here." Muse waved her hand. "It's just a bruise."

"You're exasperating with your evasive answers. I feel like pinning you down and forcing you to give it up."

Muse waggled her eyebrows. "Give what up?"

Abby jerked her head to look at Muse and blinked rapidly. "Was that an innuendo?"

Muse laughed and grabbed Abby's arm, pulling her back toward the house. "Come on. I need a shower. I'll do more practicing before we take our big ride. It can't be that hard to grind off the rust."

Abby waved her finger. "No way, I may not have a motorcycle right now, but I'm pretty sure I can ride that thing a lot better than you. And, I have a license. I'm not so sure you do. You seem to play fast and loose with the rules."

***

When Muse emerged from the shower, fully dressed, Abby's mouth hung open in surprise. Seeing Muse's classic beauty wrapped inside a tight pair of jeans and leather chaps had Abby swallowing hard.

"Um, you, uh, look amazing."

Muse held up one finger. "Oh, wait, I forgot my jacket." She pivoted and returned to the bathroom. When she emerged, a leather jacket dangled from one hand, and her saddlebag was in the other.

"I think my ultimate fantasy just materialized before my very eyes."

"I did good, huh?"

Abby nodded vigorously. "But that doesn't mean you get to drive." She held out her hand. "Gimme."

"What?"

"The keys. I'm still driving that bad girl. I even have my own helmet. I never got rid of it after my ex smashed my motorcycle. I may be a klutz, but I have never crashed. Maybe I slowly tipped over once or twice, but that doesn't count. I should probably grab a jacket, too. Although it won't be nearly anything as rad as yours. I think all I can manage is a Forks Outfitters windbreaker." Abby shrugged. "It works in a pinch."

Muse dug into her pocket and handed Abby the single key. "If we find a deserted road, will you let me drive?"

"Maybe." Abby laughed. "Goddess, look at me, getting all bossy. It's so out of character for me. I think you're a good influence."

"I am?" The level of disbelief in Muse's voice took Abby by surprise.

"Yeah, you are." Conviction draped around Abby's words.

"I haven't done a good job of inspiring for some time now. It's why I needed a vacation. I'm hoping to get my mojo back." Muse cupped her mouth and whispered, "Honestly, I have my doubts, and I wonder if I should simply let the three days lapse. Abandon my position and be done with it. But don't tell anyone I said that. Failure is not an option given to us."

"Failure is an inevitable part of everyone's life. Don't ever let anyone tell you it's not. If they do, they are lying. Granted, some, like me, experience a tad bit more than others, but still, everyone face-plants on occasion. For me, that's a literal experience more often than I'd like." Abby laughed.

"I don't think the picture of yourself is as clear as you present. An award-winning author is far from a person who has had more failure than the average bear. By the way, where does that saying come from? I don't understand it."

"You know, I'm not sure. That's one thing I haven't ever Googled. Are you stalling? Because I believe we have a date with a motorcycle, and I'm an excellent driver." Abby grinned after her robotic intonation.

Muse stared blankly at Abby.

"Aw, come on, *Rain Man*?"

"Rain Man?"

"The movie. Never mind."

"Was it about a man who makes rain?"

"How have you never heard of the movie, *Rain Man*? It was classic. Won four Academy Awards, including best picture. Not many movies featured individuals with autism before that one was released. That fact alone made it ground-breaking. The star power behind it didn't hurt. I like it when books and movies go outside the norm and make people think. I try to do that with my writing sometimes." Abby walked to her hall closet and pulled a light windbreaker from the hanger. She began to root around on the floor, pushing items aside as she searched for her helmet.

"I wouldn't know about movies. That isn't a medium that's within my purview. I agree with you on books, though."

"Editor?" Abby tossed out. She thought she would try to guess and wriggle more information from the mysterious woman.

"I do admire editors. Editing is important. Critical to the final product."

"Yes, it is. Sometimes I think a book is one part inspiration and nine parts perspiration. Stringing the actual words together and manipulating them again and again and again until it's perfect is the real work."

"Oh, I wouldn't go that far. I'd like to think inspiration plays a bigger role than only one-tenth of the final product."

"Well, if that's the case, I'm in real trouble. Right about now, I'd kill for something that causes me to drip with perspiration. Hard work is not gonna cut it this time." Finding her helmet, Abby quickly donned her jacket and grabbed the shiny black object, dangling it from her hand.

Muse smiled. "Don't worry. One way or another, inspiration will return to you. Even if that means they assign someone new."

Abby tilted her head. "You sound like a magical muse is a living breathing entity. Maybe if I had a lover who inspired me, I would be able to write again. Your name is Muse. How about you apply for the job," Abby joked.

Muse coughed. "Tempting. You'd be surprised at how the world works."

"I read somewhere that writer's block is bullshit and an excuse. A well-known author was on a panel with me once and said that she didn't have the luxury as a full-time writer to not show up to work. Just push through it, she said, and write every day because that's your job. Maybe she's correct, and maybe she's not. I hated hearing those words because I could almost feel the big L forming on my forehead, labeling me a loser. I can't push through."

"Not now, you can't, but you will. I promise. You will."

Abby jerked her head toward the front door. "Come on, I'm dying to drive a motorcycle again. Your chariot awaits."

CHAPTER SIX

"Do you trust me?" Abby turned slightly, raising her voice above the air pushing against them as they traveled on Highway 101. As long as she didn't lean back and kept resting most of her weight on her pubis versus her tailbone, she was doing okay. Earlier, she had taken four ibuprofen as insurance against the discomfort she was sure to feel during their long excursion.

"Yes, of course," Muse shouted back.

Abby wished she had a set of those headphones that allowed two people to communicate while driving sixty miles an hour down the highway. If she were honest with herself, anything past forty-five made her nervous, but Muse seemed to enjoy the speed. Everything brought joy to Muse, and that was so refreshing.

"I'm going to take you to this place that has the most amazing fresh oysters. Not because oysters are supposed to be an aphrodisiac," Abby added. "I think that's a myth." She wondered if a few of her words were lost in the wind.

"Sounds perfect."

Abby focused on the road, deciding it was better to hold off on an in-depth discussion while also concentrating on driving a motorcycle. She hadn't dared to admit that she was also a mite rusty. Clearly, her skills were not as forgotten as Muse's, making her the better choice to drive. Muse's arms wrapped snugly around her middle, and they were comforting in a way she couldn't quite put her finger on. She didn't want to overthink things. Sure, she was wildly attracted to the gorgeous woman, but there was something more hiding in the shadows.

Abby thought she needed to get out a lot more because Hama Hama Oyster Saloon was farther than she remembered. Deciding her butt needed coddling, she made several stops along the way so they could both stretch their legs. Abby had almost cruised past the first stop until Muse had tapped her shoulder and pointed to the pullout at Lake Crescent. Abby knew she'd begun to take for granted the beauty of where she lived. Muse's enthusiasm was overflowing, and some of it managed to pour into Abby's soul. Muse was off the motorcycle in a matter of seconds, looking across the lake as the sun produced picturesque sparkles on top of the placid water.

"I could spend the whole day here. Can we come back tomorrow with a picnic lunch? I'd like to have a picnic at a lake."

"Haven't you ever had a picnic in a park?" Abby dismounted less gracefully and almost performed another face-plant before catching herself at the last minute. She'd momentarily rolled back on her tailbone, and that had hurt. Fortunately, she turned away when her face contorted in pain, so Muse wouldn't notice.

Muse shook her head sadly in answer to Abby's question.

"I think a picnic lunch at Lake Crescent would be lovely. We can pick up a few delicacies on our way back for tomorrow." Abby smiled brightly. Special foods seemed like something that Muse appreciated. She'd always made an effort to shop for Jenny's favorites and stock her fridge. Now she would do the same for Muse. Maybe this time, it would make a difference.

"Oh, thank you, Abby. You're making this vacation something special, and very tough for me to go back," she gushed.

"Maybe you can extend." Abby tossed the idea out, hoping there was a chance.

"I don't believe that will be allowed."

"You could try. The only missed shot is the one you never take." Abby grimaced at her cheesy words. She'd always hated when people spouted those insidious inspirational quotes. "Sorry, forget I said that. Stupid positive sayings. How cliché."

Muse laughed. "I like that one. My favorite is it's better to ask for forgiveness than permission. He wouldn't like that, though. The consequences are a bit direr for me than for the average person."

"That sounds like a job and a boss I would not like. I'm glad I work for myself, or more accurately, my readers. I suppose I put enough pressure on myself. I don't need anyone else to add to it."

Muse grabbed Abby's hand. "Come on, let's see if we can find a path."

"I don't think this pull-off is intended for anything but viewing and pictures," Abby argued.

"Where is your sense of adventure?"

"I abandoned that many years ago after, oh, the thousandth injury. Don't forget clumsiness is my middle name. I don't pay close enough attention to my surroundings, and bam, cuts, broken bones, stuff that doesn't feel very good is the result."

"Life is risk and pain. No one can protect themselves from every injury. I'll buy you that protective plastic wrap with filled air pockets," Muse joked.

"You laugh, but I have seriously considered something like that."

"That is what must be around your heart."

Abby scrunched her face. "Huh? I haven't done that." If she'd done that, she wouldn't have made the grave error with Jenny. *What the hell was I thinking when I declared my love?*

Muse tugged Abby along, making her way closer to the water. "Do you think I can take off my shoes and dip my toes in the water? I did that on the beach, and I want to do that here."

Abby was overwhelmed with Muse's requests for such simple pleasures. The awe and hope dripped from her voice like sweet honey. "Sure, let's do it." She was starting to catch Muse's enthusiasm.

"Oh, you'll take off your boots and join me?"

Abby nodded. "Why not? You only live once."

"That's truer than you can ever imagine."

Muse's cryptic response led Abby to consider the worst possible scenario. *Could Muse have a terminal illness?*

"Muse, are you okay?" Abby scrutinized Muse, scanning her body from head to toe for any clue that she was sick. She certainly was not overweight, but she wasn't emaciated, either. Her skin did not have that grayish pallor of someone ill. In fact, the color in her cheeks was positively glowing with health. Yet, that didn't mean anything. Abby'd had a friend once who hadn't learned about her breast cancer until it was too late.

A broad smile returned to Muse's face. "Of course."

Running through the heavy vegetation along the barely visible path, the two women giggled all the way to the water. Muse plopped on the ground and pulled Abby down with her. Abby, in a usual bout of clumsiness, at least managed to land in Muse's lap, rather than on the hard ground or the prickly bush located a short distance from Muse. Muse had wrapped her arms around Abby, lightly steadying her body. By some miracle, she also hadn't landed squarely on her tailbone. Even with the soft landing that would have stung. Abby wanted to stay in Muse's arms. The closeness sent her heartbeat into overdrive. All Abby had to do was move three more inches, and her lips would meet Muse's. Instead, Abby continued to laugh, despite her awkward position, and then quickly moved to the side and began unlacing her boots. Soon after Muse had removed her shoes, she dipped a toe into the icy, clear, blue water of the lake.

"Ooh. I didn't think it would be as cold as the ocean."

Abby shifted and squinted at Muse. "I don't think many people swim in this lake or in the ocean this far north."

"That's too bad. I wanted to swim in the ocean. It's on my list."

"I'd recommend a wet suit."

"Okay, I'll get one of those—tomorrow, before I swim with the fishes and whales."

Walking carefully toward the edge of the water, Abby replied, "I'm not so sure the whales come that close to shore. No doubt, there will be fish and hopefully not any sharks."

Muse turned around, her mouth wide open. "Sharks? I don't think I would like to swim with sharks. They bite at your legs. That would hurt."

Abby chuckled. "Yes, I imagine that would. I think you'll be safe. I'll come with you. I have a wet suit from when I used to own a small ski boat and skied in the lake up in Bellingham. That lake was cold."

It hadn't occurred to Abby that having a wet suit for a three-day vacation was unusual. Since everything about Muse was slightly off, this was just another mystery she could shrug away.

***

After another stop in Sequim, the two women hit the road again and then pulled into Hama Hama Oyster Saloon. The weather continued to cooperate, prompting both women to remove their jackets, laying them on the gray wood benches around one of the matching picnic tables.

"Shall I order for us?"

"Yes." Muse nodded enthusiastically.

Muse watched Abby walk to the counter to order and thought how attractive Abby was, both from the front and the back. No wonder Muse had chosen the beach not far from Abby's home. She had to admit she was uncharacteristically focused on this particular subject. Muse was more than a little upset that Abby was experiencing such a block in her writing. She had taken that rather personally.

The frown on Muse's face lingered. When Abby returned, her bright smile evaporated, and the tiny wrinkle in Abby's forehead appeared.

"What's wrong? Oh, damn, you hate oysters, don't you? I can be so stupid sometimes. I shouldn't assume everyone likes the same foods that I do. I'll order something else. What would you like?"

"You haven't failed me yet. I would like to have oysters." Muse forced her face to relax.

"Then why were you frowning?"

"I was thinking about how I haven't managed to do my job very well lately. That disturbs me greatly."

"And what job is that?" Abby slid carefully onto the bench, lowering herself slowly.

Muse ignored her question and deftly redirected the conversation. "Why would you think I wouldn't enjoy oysters?"

"Raw oysters are an acquired taste, much like my books," Abby joked.

"Your books are very creative. They don't follow traditional themes, especially for romance. Is that not what your readers most enjoy?"

Abby shrugged. "I suppose." Abby narrowed her eyes. "Don't think you're getting away with redirecting my questions to avoid answering them. Why are you so hesitant to talk about yourself? And please don't ask me another question to send us down a rabbit trail."

Muse sighed. "I only have three days. I'd rather spend that time getting to know you. I'm not important."

"Of course, you're important. Don't I get a say in this? What if, after your vacation, I'd like to stay in touch? I don't know where you live. You've been so evasive. I can't even wiggle that tiny nugget out of you."

"We'll always be connected, but not in the way you're familiar with." Muse patted Abby's hand.

"Arghhhh. You are so exasperating. Can't you answer that one question? Where are you from? Where do you call home?" Abby shifted again, and Muse was reminded of her injury.

I'm forcing her to experience discomfort in more ways than one. Muse shook her head sadly. "Too far to continue a physical contact unless I make a radical choice. Please don't ask me any more about that. I want to enjoy my time here, not dwell on the reality of my situation."

Abby squeezed Muse's hand. "I'm sorry. I don't want to be the cause of that frown. I won't push anymore. Whatever you want to share with me is okay. I'll simply be satisfied with joining you on your journey, regardless of the short duration."

Impulsively, Muse rose halfway and leaned over, gently pecking Abby on the lips. Abby began blinking rapidly, and then a slow curve appeared at the corners of her mouth.

***

On the return to Abby's home, the two women stopped in Sequim for ice cream and a bathroom break. As Muse made her way into the bathroom, Abby stayed with the motorcycle and the various purchases they'd made along the way. Her saddlebags were no longer relatively empty as she'd stuffed them with the trinkets that she knew she could not take back with her.

When she opened the door, the woman leaning against the sink with her arms casually crossed in front startled her, saying, "Hello, Musetta. I see that your unusual name has not caused too much trouble thus far. Although, I believe Abby finds your evasiveness alluring enough to cause problems. She is clever and well-read. I wonder what Abby thinks of your name. Do you suppose she will make a connection since you are constantly dropping hints?"

Ignoring Calli's taunt, Muse stated, "You promised I would have three days. I have two more days."

Calli wagged her finger. "Not quite two more days left. Besides, that was before you began to get too close to one of the subjects. What the Hades are you thinking?" Calli nearly yelled.

Muse knew she was probably poking the bear, but she refused to answer and gave her an impertinent "whatever" look.

"I would never have authorized this vacation if I knew you were going to act so much like a love-struck human."

"What is so wrong with experiencing the very things that inspire our subjects? I believe I'll be much better at my job after my time off is complete. Besides, you were not the one who authorized my vacation."

"I most certainly was the one who convinced him this was necessary. If I hadn't gone to bat for you, this experiment would have never happened."

Muse's shoulders drooped. "I didn't know that. Thank you."

"Muse, I am worried about you. I care what happens. You're not only my protege, but I feel a great responsibility to you. I don't think you understand the consequences of dancing so close along that line. Surely you don't wish to remain here with your…subjects."

Calli's look of distress appeared so human that Muse started to giggle. "I could think of worse things. Are you experiencing your first bout of constipation?" Muse could not help making that crack. Calli's expressions kept changing and looking so familiar to what she'd seen as she watched people on the beach, in the restaurants, and out and about over the last day.

"I do not appreciate being the butt of your jokes." Calli waved her hand in the air. "You do what you want. You always have. Consider yourself warned." In a dramatic pivot, Calli turned and left the bathroom in an exaggerated huff.

After using the facilities as she had intended when she first entered the bathroom, Muse approached Abby, who looked perplexed.

"Did you say something to that woman who was in the bathroom with you? I don't think I've ever been the recipient of a more withering look. I can't imagine what you said to her. Um, did you tell her we were together? Not everyone is okay with lesbians, I guess. It's become so much worse with our current president. Sorry, I'm rambling."

"Don't worry about it. Maybe she had something to eat that affected her. Constipation can be very painful." Muse giggled again.

Abby wrinkled her nose. "I think we're too young to start discussing bodily functions. What will we talk about when we turn seventy?"

"You are very funny."

"I better head to the bathroom before I wet my drawers like someone a lot older than seventy, and then we can head to the ice cream shop. You're going to love their lavender ice cream. It's to die for. Usually, I stock my freezer with Ben and Jerry's chocolate chip cookie dough, but the lavender flavor is so unusual, it's worth it to cheat on Ben and Jerry. I can't be faulted for my lack of loyalty if they don't offer lavender as a flavor."

"I would love to try both. Thank you, Abby."

***

Abby smiled when she saw Plato looking warily at the two women as he perched himself on top of the refrigerator. She knew that eventually, his curiosity would get the better of him, and he would inch a bit closer. That might take another hour or another day. Cats were fickle, and Plato was the epitome of the aloof stereotype—until he decided it was time to make friends.

Abby had made eye contact with him, letting him know she knew his game with his half-closed lids as he pretended not to notice Muse. She almost called him on his game and reached up to pet him, but then he'd probably run and hide. Muse watched the interaction, and Abby thought she saw longing in her eyes. Yearning for what, she didn't know. Plato barely twitched a muscle as Abby retrieved the wine from the refrigerator. She let him be for now.

Gingerly lowering her sore behind on the loveseat in her living room, Abby raised her glass in the air and then sipped her wine. She had poured two glasses and was eager to sit on something that wasn't hard and vibrating, even if she'd managed to avoid pressure on her tailbone by leaning forward the whole time. Not that she didn't appreciate certain hard, vibrating items strategically placed on her sensitive bits, but a motorcycle for several hours was not one of them.

"Ahhh. Why can't motorcycle seats have memory foam or something a lot softer than the cushions of Satan?"

Muse choked on the wine she'd just sipped. "Cushions of Satan? I don't think I've ever heard that term for a bike seat."

"I guess it doesn't go with the macho or macha connected to motorcycle owners. Y'all have to be a bunch of badasses, don't you? Maybe that's why I don't own one anymore. I get in enough trouble on my own. I've injured my ass plenty without taking a long ride on a motorcycle." Abby narrowed her eyes. "Why aren't you sore? You can't convince me you've spent hours on that evil thing."

Muse shrugged. "I'm a little sore, I guess. Maybe riding bitch is more comfortable. Besides, I'm not the one who injured her tailbone."

Abby erupted with laughter. "Okay, I know you had to force that from your mouth. Riding bitch? Really? I don't think my soreness has much to do with my tailbone. I managed to avoid pressure on that particular spot most of the ride."

"Tell me about your past loves."

The new direction Muse took in the conversation was abrupt, but Abby was used to Muse leading them down a completely different path.

"Those will be boring tales. You don't want to hear about my exes."

"Yes, I do. How about your first love? That's usually safe to ask about."

Abby sighed. "Ah, Penny Lane. Yes, that really was her name. She had this string of freckles across her nose, even though she always sported a deep tan in the summer."

"Freckles are attractive?"

"Yeah, I guess they were to me. Sometimes they still are. There's something so innocent and youthful about freckles, especially when they appear on a person in their mid-forties. Dimples have the same effect on me. I'm a sucker for freckles and dimples."

"How old was this new freckle-faced beauty?"

Abby catapulted back in time to her youth, and ironically, she didn't mind taking that trip. "We were twelve. At the time, I didn't think too much about how I hung on her every word. I would imagine she didn't either. Although I'd love to know what happened to her. I'd like to think she turned out to be a lesbian or maybe bisexual. I'll never know." As she stared into space, Abby became silent.

"Was Penny your first kiss?"

Abby's head snapped back, and she met Muse's eyes as Muse propped her head on her hand.

"Oh, goodness, no. My first kiss was with a boy who everyone else, except Penny, insisted I should declare as my boyfriend. He sent a messenger to feel me out, and that messenger thought he was dreamy. I didn't. But peer pressure was alive and well at the time."

Muse picked up her wine, took a sip, and leaned back. "Tell me about the kiss."

"Not much to tell. A version of spin the bottle where we were totally set up and put inside a closet. We counted to ten and then awkwardly pressed our lips together. I don't remember wishing the bottle would have landed on Penny, but I knew Joe wasn't doing it for me. Our relationship, if you could call it that, lasted a whole month." Abby laughed. "Your turn to tell me about your first kiss. Come on. Throw me a bone here, please?"

"You were there. Not much of a story, I suppose."

Abby opened her mouth, but no words would come out. Muse had to be joking. "What?" Abby asked in disbelief.

"You were my first kiss, Abby."

Trying to lighten the suddenly awkward mood, Abby asked, "Did you grow up in a convent?" She slapped her hand against her thigh. "Oh, my Goddess. I kissed a nun. Wait. You kissed me."

"I did." Muse grinned. "Should I do it again?"

"Not if you're a nun. That's just…" Abby shifted again on the couch, but this time it was related to her discomfort, thinking about defiling a nun.

"I've read about lesbian nuns."

"So that's why you've been so tight-lipped. You're running away from your vows. I feel like I'm in the middle of a lesbian version of *The Sound of Music*. Except, I'm no dashing captain, and I definitely can't hold a tune. Can you?"

Muse shrugged. "Don't know. I haven't tried that yet. Tell me about your first kiss with a girl or woman."

"Nice redirect. Fine. I'll jump back onto your page, as long as I get you talking more about your experience as a nun. That's fascinating to me."

Muse smiled but didn't respond, and the silence became uncomfortable to Abby. "It was a woman. I was a late bloomer. Penny moved away before we hit high school and the hormones kicked in. I let my other friends, who were all very straight, lead me down the straight and narrow path. But after I finished graduate school, I met a woman who probably had very refined gaydar, and she took charge."

"I want to hear the story."

"I met her when in-person book clubs were a thing. People got together at someone's house and talked about whatever book the group had decided to read. Nowadays, most of that is done online. I miss the old days, but I live too far from civilization now."

"Okay, so you met her at a book club meeting," Muse prompted.

"We were reading *Yellow Raft in Blue Water* at the time, and she got that glint in her eye I came to know well. She suggested *Confessions of a Failed Southern Lady* because it was one of the funniest books she'd ever read, and she thought it was about time our little group started reading something a bit lighter. I agreed. I wanted to lighten up the group as well."

"I haven't read either book," Muse admitted.

"Oh, you should. I highly recommend both of those books. I used to have them in paperback, but every single time I bought a new copy, I kept lending them to people and never getting them back. Now I have them both in an e-book version."

"You're stalling. Get to the good part already." Muse grinned.

"Well, she caught me after the book club ended and said she could tell we were kindred spirits. We set a time and date to meet on the coming Saturday. She wanted me to have an opportunity to start the book before we got together."

"Do all writers take forever to tell a story?" Muse joked.

"Fine. I read the book. My eyes were opened. We kissed. End of story."

"If I promise not to complain anymore, can you please fill in a few blanks for me?" Muse batted her eyes.

Abby chuckled. "That look right there" —Abby pointed to Muse— "used to be her signature move as well. Whenever she wanted something. The book was about a woman exploring her sexuality. Then she entered into a relationship with a woman despite her southern upbringing. It was hilarious. I was bold and asked her if she was a lesbian. She didn't miss a beat and proceeded to ask me what I would do if she kissed me."

"Really? At least she asked you before she planted her lips on yours."

Abby shook her head. "True. I stuttered something like, 'I don't know.' To her, that meant 'sure, go ahead.' She didn't waste time. I remember thinking about the softness of her lips. But I made the grave error of telling her it didn't feel a lot different from kissing a man. I'd intended to pass it off as no big deal that a woman had kissed me for the first time. Although the kiss was far from chaste. I think I remember a little tongue action. Your turn. Tell me what it's like to be a nun."

"I'm not a nun."

CHAPTER SEVEN

Abby puffed her cheeks. She thought she had it all figured out. Muse was sheltered, and if she were honest, a bit on the eccentric side, so the narrative of her being a nun had fit quite nicely.

"Muse, are we friends?"

"That's a hard question to answer because the definition of friends seems different to different people."

"You're one of the most exasperating women I have ever met." A blast of air burst from Abby's mouth in a cross between a huff and a scoff.

"Tell me what a friend means to you. And tell me if that's what you want us to be. I need your complete candor."

Muse took Abby's hand, and the sincerity of her look touched Abby in a place she didn't think anyone had ever wakened before. There was something so raw and vulnerable in the way she made this simple request of Abby.

Abby paused to gather her thoughts. As she reasoned through what Muse wanted to know, she realized how difficult it was to describe what a friend means. But what felt impossible was answering Muse's next question. If Abby were honest, a friend didn't go nearly as far as she wanted. She'd been there and done that with Jenny. Physical intimacy wasn't the only thing she longed for. She wanted the emotional connection to someone who would be there for her day in and day out. Abby needed that special person to help her meet the challenges and ups and downs of a life together. A best friend fell short of that. She could admit that to herself, but could she confess that to Muse?

"I concede friendship is hard to define. I haven't had many true friends in my life. When I have had them, I intuitively know they've met that definition. They certainly have shared a few traits. Number one is they've stuck by me no matter what stupid thing came out of my mouth. That doesn't mean I've gotten a full pass. A friend has to be honest, even if it hurts. A friend trusts me with information that's so private they know I'll never break their trust and vice versa. Finally, no matter how many months go by, if I call and need them, they do whatever is necessary to be there with me."

"Like what? What have friends done to be there with you?"

"Middle of the night calls to calm me. Hours of travel to sit with me when I've been at my lowest. I don't have to express everything for them to understand what I'm thinking and feeling. They just know."

"What about if they are always there with you, even when you can't see, hear, or feel their physical presence?" Muse kept her penetrating gaze on Abby.

"Muse, have you had a friend pass away? Is that what you're talking about?"

"Not exactly. My vacation ends in less than two days." Muse removed her hand. Her eyes contained such sorrow that Abby wanted to wrap her body into a hug that would take away whatever pain had wormed its way inside her soul.

"I don't know if I can meet those expectations. I don't believe that would be allowed."

"Allowed? You're speaking in riddles again."

"If there were limitations, would you still wish to have a friendship?"

This time Abby grabbed Muse's hand. She sucked in air and tentatively proceeded. If she were honest, she wanted more than friendship. "No, I don't want a friendship."

Muse jerked her hand away for the second time and stood. "I understand."

Abby moved quickly to re-establish her connection to Muse. She pulled Muse's body close to her and turned Muse's face around to make Muse look at her. "I want so much more than friendship." Bringing their lips together, Abby deepened the kiss when she didn't feel any resistance from Muse. Her tongue slipped effortlessly inside as one hand moved to Muse's face, and the other found its way to the small of her back.

A barely audible moan escaped from Muse's lips. When the two women broke apart, Muse smiled. "I hope a story will evolve from this kiss, even if it isn't your first."

"Let me help you, Muse. If you're running away from something, I hope you feel you can trust me."

"I'm not in danger if that's what you think."

"Then what?" Abby asked, more harshly than she intended. "You're going to walk out of my life in less than two days, and I can't do a thing about it. You won't even tell me how to find you or keep in touch. Surely you feel the same connection as I do." She scrubbed her hand over her face.

Muse touched Abby on the shoulder and gently led her to the couch. "Come, sit. Can't we simply enjoy the here and now?"

"Dying. You're dying. That's it." Abby knew she was reaching for straws, but maybe one of the darts she tossed at the target would hit. If she launched enough of them with gusto, perhaps one of her guesses would land in the center.

Throwing her head back, Muse laughed without restraint. "I am not dying. Your understanding of life, death, the universe is quite narrow, and limited to what you can see, hear, smell, and touch. Perhaps there is an expansion of those traditional views of intelligent life."

Abby furrowed her brow. "Okay, I know I've written about aliens, and I suppose I think there may be life on other galaxies. Surely, you're not claiming to be some kind of alien. That's just…"

Muse smiled. "No, not an alien, but you've just illustrated my point. Even the most open-minded person restricts their notion of possibilities. I'm sure you believe as a writer of romance combined with paranormal, science fiction, and fantasy, you have all the answers about what might be out there." Muse shook her head. "I've very much admired your imagination, but even you put a box around the world. Limitations are in your nature, and lately, you've let them rule, and I've failed miserably in removing them."

"I don't understand."

Muse jumped from the couch. "I'm hungry. Can we get pizza, please?"

Abby knew it did zero good to try to get Muse to continue on a conversation path after she'd executed her abrupt subject-change maneuver. She rubbed her behind. "All right, can we take my car, please? I don't think my bottom can take another minute on your motorcycle. I'll endure the thirty-minute trip by sitting on one butt cheek. That ought to work for me."

***

Abby seemed to know everyone at Pacific Pizza. The place was packed, and Muse didn't know if that was because it was literally the only pizza place for miles, or the food was that good. She'd find out soon enough.

"This place seems popular."

"There isn't a lot to choose from unless you want to travel a fair distance. But actually, this place is good. I think you'll like their pizza." Abby reached the front counter and initially smiled, then coughed in apparent discomfort. "Hey, Nat. How's it going? I hear you're heading to UW next year. Good for you."

"Yeah, I'm excited. Mom is over the moon. You should come by sometime. She misses you."

"Um, I don't think that's a very good idea." Abby shuffled her feet, and Muse definitely registered that Abby had reacted strangely to the young woman.

"Mom told me what happened. She's not mad or anything."

Abby's face turned red. "Ugh. Not one of my better moments. Sometimes I'm too honest for my own good."

"She's just, you know, kinda closed off. Thank God I'm part of a newer generation that can explore stuff. I feel sorry for old people."

"Hey, who you calling old? I'll call, I promise. Your mom and I have been friends for a long time. I just need to get over my mortification."

Nat turned her focus to Muse and gave her the once over. "Wow, Abby, who's your friend? She's hot."

"Seriously, Nat. You did not just say that. What about us being old?"

"Hey, I can appreciate a beautiful woman regardless of age. See, there's the difference between my generation and yours. We aren't uptight about stuff like that."

Muse reached across the counter with her outstretched hand. "Hi, I'm Muse. It seems like Abby has been keeping a few stories very close to her vest." Muse quirked her eyebrow.

"Ooh, jealousy. Yeah, that's not part of our generation either. Don't worry, Mom and Abby are just friends. Although Abby kinda confessed she had other feelings. Mom's too uptight to go for it. I wish she would have. It would have been so cool to say my mom was dating a famous writer. Instead, she's dating boring old David. Oops." Nat slapped her hand against her mouth.

"David? Jenny hasn't talked about anyone named David." Abby's voice cracked with emotion.

"I'm sorry, Abby, I know she was going to and then…"

Abby shook her head and turned to Muse. "Um, Muse, what kind of pizza would you like?"

Muse chuckled and whispered in Abby's ear, "Now who's redirecting?" Muse turned her face toward Nat. "I'm open to anything. What would you recommend, Nat?"

Nat looked at Abby. "Want your usual, then?"

"Nope, I'm going to prove you wrong, Nat. You know, open myself to other possibilities. How about we take a large barbecue chicken and pineapple?" Abby suggested.

"Rad. Interesting combination." Nat waggled her eyebrows. "Hey, I read somewhere that when you eat a pineapple, you taste like—"

"Do not finish that sentence," Abby warned.

Nat pointed to Abby's forehead. "Plato trip you again?"

Abby touched the small cut that Muse had tended to. She'd almost forgot about the injury. The event seemed so long ago. "No, just being my typical clumsy self."

"You need to wrap yourself in bubble wrap. Mom says she worries about you living alone so far from town. She does care about you, you know. Just maybe not in the way that you want."

"Hey, there's a line forming." Abby handed Nat her credit card. "I promise I'll pull up my granny panties and call her next week."

Nat wrinkled her nose. "You don't really wear granny panties, do you? I thought you might be cool and like, wear boi shorts."

Abby turned her head as another couple stepped behind the girl and boy, who were now giggling behind Abby. "Seriously? I will not talk to you about my choice of underwear while a line forms behind me. Next thing you know, it'll be the headline in the Forks Forum."

Nat efficiently ran Abby's credit card and handed it back to her. "You are seriously fun to wind up." She nodded at the couple standing behind Abby and Muse. "Hey, Connor, hey, Sarah. What's up?"

After shoving her credit card back inside the rubber holder attached to the back of her phone, Abby grabbed Muse's arm and whispered, "Time to make our escape while she's distracted."

"Only if I get to hear the story of Nat's mom." Muse grinned.

Abby sighed and grabbed the table marker.

***

Abby picked up her glass of water and took a nervous sip. "I don't suppose you're going to let this go and forget that whole embarrassing exchange at the counter."

"Not even a remote chance of that happening. Were you or are you in love with Nat's mom?"

"Hmm. That's a complicated question with an even more convoluted answer."

"You're a storyteller. I'm sure you can manage to give me sufficient details to understand."

"Jenny and I were friends in high school. We both went off to college and lost touch for several years. She married. I didn't. Both of us missed living in a small town. It wasn't hard for her to return because she married a doctor, and they always seem to need physicians in Forks." Abby rested her hands on the wood table.

"I don't see you getting involved with a married woman. That doesn't fit."

"Oh, no, I would never. Jenny is divorced now. Her cheating slimebag of a husband had an affair with a nurse, and they moved to PA."

"PA?" Muse asked.

"Port Angeles. Far enough away to let him still see his daughter, but enough distance that it wasn't salt in Jenny's wounds every single day. We got tight again after the divorce. I was kind of her shoulder to cry on. We had rekindled our friendship before the divorce when she moved back, but we got a lot closer afterward. I misread the signals." Abby shrugged. "That's all."

"That doesn't sound convoluted. Nor do I think that's the whole story."

"Nat's a great kid. Honestly, I think what I fell in love with was the closeness. It almost felt like we were a family, without the side benefit of sex. It was comfortable for all of us." Abby glanced toward the counter at Nat. "I let the whole experience send me down a road I never should have taken. Jenny does not see me as a potential partner. She sees me as her best friend—as the person who, in her words, 'saved her wretched life.' I filled a vacuum. She did, as well. But, neither of us plugged the void."

"Friendship is often the basis for deeper relationships. Start as friends and evolve to something more. Right?" Muse asked.

"Not always. Actually, not very often in my experience. Deep down, I knew it wasn't what either one of us needed or wanted. I was simply so sick and tired of being alone. I already have a solitary job. Not having someone to confide in, to be there every day to ask about your day, to patch you when you fall, which is quite often for me, was killing me. Jenny did a lot of that for me. And yet, there was something big missing." Abby began nervously clasping and unclasping her fingers together as her hands remained on the table.

"Sex?" Muse took one of Abby's hands, and Abby let her.

"Sure, sex is a big part, but for me, it's the intimacy that I connect to sex. Physical intimacy takes the relationship to that next level for me. Jenny and I had everything but that."

Muse nodded. "I've read your books, and that's how you portray the sex scenes. I prefer that in the romance books I read. I like those better than erotica."

Abby tilted her head. "You read erotica?"

"Sure, I read everything my subjects write. How else will I know…"

"Aha, you *are* an editor. I knew it! I know that some writers are hermits. Are editors prone to that life? I guess editing can be a solo job as well. You don't have to interact with anyone but the authors and publishers. That can be done via computer interchanges."

Muse wondered how wrong it was to let Abby continue to believe she was an editor. It was getting harder for her not to spill the beans. "Will you excuse me, please, I need to use the restroom."

Abby pointed to a hallway. "It's through there."

***

Calli leaned casually against the sink. "Don't do it, Muse."

Muse pushed past her. "Don't do what?"

"Don't tell her who you are. It's bad enough that social media is nearly blowing up right now with thousands of posts on authors experiencing the worst writer's block they've ever had in their entire life. You know this holiday you're on is putting everything in jeopardy. I can't believe how selfish you're acting."

"Everyone and everything can be replaced. I wasn't doing a very good job before. Can't you see how necessary this was for me?"

"No, I can't. Do you honestly believe that a periodic block here and there with your subjects is a huge catastrophe? It happens. Get over it. Right now, you're causing a massive wave. There is no inspiration in the entire Pacific Northwest. That's the true disaster. What if this catastrophe spreads? Why were you so worried about this particular subject?"

"I don't know. I just know what I'm doing now is the right thing."

"What about if we inspire her to move to another territory? Then you won't have to worry anymore. She won't be one of your subjects." Calli brushed her hands together. "Problem solved."

"No, no, don't do that. I promise I'll figure it out," Muse pleaded.

Calli's eyes softened. "You really care for this one, don't you?"

Muse turned on the faucet and splashed cold water on her face, pausing before answering. "Has this ever happened before?"

Calli shrugged. "Not quite in the same way, but yes…there were maybe a handful of others. I know you heard about Death, too. He had a kind of crisis a long time ago. He dealt with it."

"That's so…morbid," Muse deadpanned.

Calli laughed. "A joke? She is rubbing off on you."

"Yeah, I did hear something about that."

"He was a bit stiff, but I guess he had a similar experience. You know, a lot of firsts for him, too." Calli had a faraway look in her eyes.

"Calli, I know you've been my mentor, but don't you think it's possible to be better at what we do if we can experience those emotions firsthand?"

"I don't know, Muse. It comes at such a high price." The worried expression on Calli's face was out of the norm for her usual stoic mentor.

"Nothing worth having is without a cost." Muse pinned Calli with a determined look.

"It was different with Death. He was alone. You are not."

"No, I'm not alone right now, but I was, Calli. I'm not like you and the others. For an unknown reason, I'm different, and I've got to figure out why."

"You're not that different," Calli mumbled. "Besides, Death wanted to know why people feared him. We aren't feared, we're depended on."

"People depend on Death. Sometimes it's the only thing that can take away the pain."

"Stop being so maudlin and serious. No wonder you had a hard time doing your job," Calli chastised.

"You aren't helping. And, you certainly aren't making a convincing argument to return before my three days are finished." Muse moved to the wall and rested her head against the cold tile.

"Muse, your appearance is adding to Abby's confusion. I understand how appealing we can be. Objectively, this" — Calli gestured to Muse's form— "is very hard to resist. You know it ended badly for Death."

"Did it?"

Calli nodded.

Muse shook her head. "I don't think so. I thought he got what he came for. He found love. That's everything. All the versions of the story I heard had that one fact in common. Even when the woman stayed behind.”

“Stop romanticizing this vacation. It’s not real.” Calli crossed her arms.

“Oh, but you’re wrong, Calli. Very wrong. I still have more time. Please let me enjoy it. You’re cramping my style by popping in uninvited and raining on my parade.”

“Oh, please. Stop with the colloquiums.” Calli held up her hand. “Or pick more inventive ones.”

“I think you mean aphorisms. Don’t you ever read what your subjects write?”

“No. Whatever,” Calli scoffed.

“Slang. I’m impressed.” Muse grinned.

“This is so uncomfortable. I don’t like coming down here. It makes me say and do ridiculous things. Now I’m talking smack like my subjects.”

“Oh, come on. Isn’t it just a little fun? By the way, who inspired those different versions of the story with Death, and which one was true?”

“You know, I don’t actually know the answer. I’ll ask. Now I’m curious.” Calli groaned. “I’ve got to get out of here before this virus or whatever it is takes over, and I end up like you. Flings are one thing, but deeper feelings are dangerous. See you in less than two days, Muse. Don’t be late.” Calli patted her arm and walked out of the bathroom. Muse hoped she wouldn’t cause a scene and do something stupid like approach Abby. She did not need this shit.

***

Muse looked upset as she slid into the booth, grumbling under her breath. "It's not like there's only one of us. Calli should mind her own damn business."

"What?" Abby stared at Muse. She'd never seen her quite like this, except one time in the very beginning, when Abby had made that joke about her inspiration taking the form of a high school mean girl. "Did something happen in the restroom to upset you? Tell me who was cruel. I'll punch their lights out, pull their hair, or something equally horrific."

Muse giggled. "Sorry. It was nothing. Just a pesky colleague trying to be helpful."

"You got a call from one of your authors? We can be such prima donnas. Always resisting helpful suggestions. You have to understand that our writing is our baby sometimes. We can't be objective when someone says our baby is ugly and needs a makeover. Did you get a phone call? My editor is smart enough not to give me her phone number, but I've been known to send private messages when she doesn't answer my emails."

Nat coughed when she laid the pizza on the table. "Um, Abby, don't be mad, okay?"

"Why would I be mad? Did you burn the pizza?"

"No, uh, she was so lost." Nat dropped her head and stared at her feet.

Abby turned her head as Jenny purposefully made her way to the table. "I'm not letting you get away with avoiding me forever. And how dare you not tell your best friend about the new woman in your life? Scootch over."

"Hey, Mom. I gotta head back to the register. Greg is giving me the stink eye." Nat walked quickly to the counter.

Abby groaned and slid to the left while Jenny glided into the booth. She turned her bright blue eyes in Muse's direction and gave her the once over. Before Jenny could attack, Abby went on the defensive.

"Oh, would that be like not telling me about David?"

Jenny waved off her pointed question. "Not important right now." She focused her attention on Muse. "Well, my daughter was right. You are attractive." She held out her hand. "I'm Jenny, and you are?"

Muse shook Jenny's hand. "Muse."

"Right. And who are you? How long have you known Abby, and why haven't I heard a single thing about you?"

"I only met Muse yesterday on the beach. Stop grilling her, okay? And, you have no reason to talk. I'm bringing up the unimportant David."

Jenny narrowed her eyes and ignored Abby's statement. "Are you two sleeping together?"

"No!" Abby exclaimed.

"Why not? If I was a lesbian, which I believe we've already determined I'm not, she would certainly get my juices flowing. Unfortunately, that fact did not exactly reveal itself in the manner that I would have liked. But, God, Abby, I could also be converted…oh, wait, not that you aren't gorgeous. You know what I mean. I would jump all over that." Jenny gestured to Muse.

"I like her," Muse declared.

"Well, great, then it's settled. Take the pizza to go. Nat, get a box for them," Jenny shouted to her daughter.

"No, I meant, I like you. Very direct."

"Oh. You don't like Abby?" Jenny pursed her lips.

"Oh no, I am very fond of Abby as well."

"Um, I believe we've already established I'm not gay, bi, or whatever, despite my daughter's lectures on closing myself to possibilities. Sorry, no threesome for me."

Muse grinned. "I see why you wanted more from Jenny. She is funny, like you."

"I believe we have finally broken through that invisible barrier to complete awkwardness. I'm sorry, Jenny. I needed time. I wasn't going to ignore you forever."

Jenny waved her hand in the air again. "Right, right, apology accepted as long as you two come for dinner tomorrow night. We'll have a double date."

Abby jerked her head in Jenny's direction and looked her square in the eye. "So now I'm allowed to hear about the elusive David. Why didn't you tell me you'd met someone?"

Jenny draped her arm around Abby and squeezed. "Oh, hon, I'm not as clueless as you think I am. I knew you had, uh, feelings for me before our talk. How could I not? I wasn't about to tell you about him after you laid yourself bare."

Muse's lips formed a straight line, and Abby wondered why her normally free-spirited new friend was almost frowning. Her unwavering gaze was so thorough, she appeared to scrutinize Jenny as if she were a bug under a microscope. Abby didn't have the energy to figure out what was going on with Muse while her mortal embarrassment was taking hold.

Abby groaned and smacked her head on the table. "I'm an idiot."

For the first time, when Jenny rubbed her back, it didn't drive Abby crazy. So often in the past, without realizing Abby's response, her affectionate friend had used physical gestures of support or comfort.

"I didn't want to tell you about David until the time was right. We met online. Still early days, but he's pretty special to me."

When Abby lifted her head, she caught Muse's horrified look. "Yup, I'm a total loser. Run. Fast and far."

"No, no, you are *not* a loser." Muse began desperately removing napkins from the dispenser and shoving them in Abby's direction. "You opened your wound. It's bleeding."

Abby bumped her best friend. "Will you excuse me, please? It seems like I need to attend to my cut before I bleed all over this table." She touched her forehead and felt the familiar wetness. The red droplets landed on the table like colorful raindrops until she pushed a handful of napkins against her head.

***

Muse followed Abby into the bathroom. She was worried about her. Not knowing Abby very well, Muse wasn't sure how she normally reacted to her friend showing up. The news that Jenny was dating had to be hard. Muse didn't know if it was a bruised ego, embarrassment, or sadness that was running the show. Abby was hard to read at the moment. She knew this situation was uncomfortable, but the specific reasons eluded Muse.

"We should get Nat to pack up the pizza and take it back to your place. I think I can manage to superglue your wound again."

"Yeah. I think that will work. Sorry for ruining your evening." Abby turned on the cold water faucet to wet the napkins she held tightly against her forehead, without looking in the mirror.

"You haven't ruined my evening one bit. Do you think we should have sex? Your friend seems to think so."

Abby began choking on air as she continued to press the napkins against her wound. "Uh, sorry. Could we have this conversation in another location? The bathroom seems a little skeevy to me. I need a proper glass of wine, maybe the whole bottle before we go there?"

"You mean before we have sex?" Muse was confused.

"No, I mean before we talk about it." Abby breathed deeply, and it seemed like she was trying to ground herself.

"Okay," Muse answered cheerily.

"Should we invite your friend? The pizza looks plentiful." Muse wanted nothing more than to learn additional facts about Abby, and that source of knowledge was waiting for them in the restaurant.

"I don't think that's the best idea right now. Especially if we want to have a serious discussion." Removing the soiled napkins from her wound, Abby turned to the mirror to inspect the injury. "It looks like the bleeding has slowed."

Muse leaned in to get a better look. "I think you're right, but maybe a reapplication of glue won't hurt. You know, Jenny will need to return to her home at some point, and then we can talk about sex. She seems to have an opinion that perhaps we should explore." Muse grinned.

"Um, definitely not. Jenny's opinion does not hold any weight," Abby huffed.

"It doesn't? I thought she was your best friend."

"She is, but that doesn't give her the right to make decisions on who I have sex with and when that might happen." Abby tossed the soiled napkins in the wastebasket and put her hands on her hips.

"Unless it was with her, right?" Muse felt an uncomfortable twinge.

"Um, yeah, but you know that is not a possibility. Ever." Abby seemed to deflate as she relaxed her posture and let her hands fall to her sides.

"Is it terrible for me to say that I'm glad?" Something was happening inside, and Muse did not enjoy this feeling. It felt black and dark.

Abby furrowed her brow. "You are?"

"I think I might be jealous. What does jealousy feel like? It does not feel green." Muse noticed a red bubble appear again and tugged on the paper towel dispenser to use against the cut.

Abby appeared to lean into Muse's touch as Muse gently dabbed at the wound. "I suppose it's like your question about friendship. I don't know that the experience is the same for everyone."

"What is it like for you? Are you jealous of this David person?" Muse stepped away but remained ready to minister to Abby's injury should it start to bleed again.

Abby slumped against the sink and nodded. "Yeah, I guess I am. When Nat first mentioned him, I developed this fluttering in my stomach like when an elevator drops too quickly. It feels like anxiety. For me, the two go hand in hand."

Muse touched her stomach. "It felt like something dense landed inside my stomach. Is that what people mean when they describe a pit in their belly? Do you think I'm jealous?" Muse tossed the soiled paper towel into the garbage.

Abby shrugged. "Maybe, or maybe you're anxious or uncomfortable. You don't strike me as a particularly nervous person, but that's what I feel like when I'm anxious. I can make an excuse not to go to dinner with Jenny and her new love if you want."

"No, I don't think we should do that. I want to learn more about this Jenny person. I want to know why you love her," Muse declared.

The door opened, and Jenny poked her head inside. "Hey, I thought you two must have drowned in there. Nat brought a box, and everything is packed and ready to go. I'll follow you. It's my turn to make the drive to your house. Besides, I don't have your special glue to fix that nasty cut, even though it looks a lot better."

"Um, you don't have to come over." Abby looked down at her feet, avoiding Jenny's gaze.

"Of course I do. I'm starving and eager to try that new combination you ordered. You must be a good influence if you got this one to try something new." Jenny gestured to Abby with her thumb. "It'll be just us gals tonight. No testosterone to muck up the evening. We'll get plenty of that tomorrow night." Jenny shut the door leaving Muse and Abby in the bathroom, looking at one another.

Abby sighed. "I guess we don't have much choice. Do we?"

"There's always a choice. I will control the pit tonight if you can stop the elevator tomorrow night." Muse held out her hand. "Deal?"

"Sure, why not?" Abby's lips barely curled into a smile. Muse wanted desperately for the real smile to return. She didn't know anymore if her insistence on keeping the dinner date to learn more about Jenny was such a good idea.

"That doesn't mean we won't have the sex talk later." Calli would probably chastise her again if she had sex with Abby, but she didn't care because this might be her only chance, and damned if she was going to blow it.

Abby groaned. "Can't wait."

CHAPTER EIGHT

Muse made quick work of reapplying the Super Glue. Afterward, Jenny and Muse sat on the couch, chattering away like they'd been friends forever. Abby didn't believe wine paired well with pizza. She'd always preferred beer or a hard cider. Since her beer-drinking days had long since passed, Abby reached into the refrigerator and pulled three hard ciders from the rack. Juggling the beverages was not a talent she possessed, and so she promptly dropped one, which landed squarely on her little toe.

"Shit, fuck, fuck!" Having met the soft tissue to break the fall, the bottle miraculously stayed intact but rolled across the smooth floor while Abby hopped up and down.

"Abby? Did you hurt yourself again?" Jenny asked.

"Meow." Plato, who had been absent over the last day while a stranger invaded his territory, wove himself between her legs after she stopped jumping around on one leg like a madwoman. Abby suspected he only came out because his favorite human, Jenny, had entered the house.

Concern swept across Muse's face as she walked over and lent Abby her body to lean on while Abby hobbled to the couch. Jenny held her hands out to gather the remaining ciders. She picked up the third, which came to a stop against the baseboard on the kitchen's far wall.

After removing Abby's sock, Muse declared, "I'm no expert, but you probably broke your toe. Shall we go to the emergency room?"

Abby flicked her hand. "Nah, this is not my first rodeo. There isn't a lot they can do for a broken toe."

"I think Abby's broken every bone at least once. In high school, she wasn't the last picked because she couldn't hit the ball or make a basket. She was the last picked because she always got hurt. It was her special talent." Jenny offered this commentary as if it wasn't something Abby should feel embarrassment over. As if it were all part of her charm. "She could have milked that for all it was worth. Guys eat up the vulnerable ones. Abby didn't like guys and was oblivious to the girls. The athletes might not have wanted her on their team, but they sure wanted to kiss her." Jenny winked.

"Except you," Abby mumbled, too low for anyone to hear. Muse looked up, and her expression telegraphed that she had heard. The frown reappeared, and Abby felt terrible for causing Muse any discomfort.

"Your cat is gorgeous," Muse remarked. Abby knew Muse well enough to know this was another conversation redirect. She swelled with a feeling of warmth at recognizing Muse was doing this on Abby's behalf. Clearly picking up on Abby's discomfort, she'd distracted Jenny.

After Plato rolled over for her, Jenny ran her hand over his back and scratched under his chin. "Yes, he is a handsome boy. Aren't you, buddy?"

"I'll be fine, Muse," Abby said. "Let's eat before the pizza gets so cold that we'll think it's the next morning after we've drunk so much, we're all hung over, and grabbing for the leftover pizza without bothering to heat it."

"Ooh, yeah. Let's do a sleepover like in high school. I'm feeling the need to recapture my youth. Unless you have a romantic evening planned. Oh, shit, am I horning in?"

"Yes." Muse narrowed her eyes.

"No!" Abby exclaimed at the same time.

Jenny looked between the two women, and their faces turned to one another. "Um, I have this thing I have to do later. I almost forgot." Jenny smiled. "Muse, where are you from and tell me about this meeting on the beach?"

"Muse is strategically tight-lipped about herself. I'm interested in this answer as well." Abby smiled.

"I don't have one place. My territory is the Pacific Northwest," Muse replied.

"I've never met an editor who travels to the author and works with them face-to-face. Talk about gold star service." Abby picked up her cider and took a long pull from the bottle.

"Not that your editor is crap, Abby, but you should hire Muse, especially if she makes office calls." Jenny grinned as she grabbed a piece of pizza and took a large bite.

"Jenny, what do you do for a living?" Once again, Muse had deftly led Jenny in a different direction.

"I'm an ultrasound tech."

"Is that how you met your ex-husband?" Muse asked.

Abby wondered for a brief moment if this was an innocent question or was Muse purposely needling her best friend. She couldn't tell.

"Yes. The rat bastard. He was a poor struggling med student when I met him. I was the one who paid the bills while he finished med school."

"At least you had a good lawyer, and the divorce settlement was quite generous." Abby wanted to remind Jenny of how she'd taken her ex to the cleaners. That always seemed to brighten her mood.

"Yeah." Jenny smiled. "He's still up to his eyeballs in debt now. I hear they live in a tiny bungalow because it's all he can afford."

"Nat seems like a nice young woman," Muse tossed into the conversation.

"Oh, yes. She is. Nat is the one good thing to come from our marriage. Are you two going to continue seeing one another? You make a beautiful couple."

Abby chuckled to herself, recognizing that Jenny was not an easy person to redirect.

Muse looked away, and Abby saw her eyes fill with water. Something was definitely amiss. She narrowed her eyes at Jenny and gave a slight shake of her head. "Anyone want another cider?"

Abby started to get up, but Muse placed her hand on Abby's thigh. "I'll get it."

"Um, none for me. I have to go soon and need to set a good example. One is my limit if I'm going to get behind the wheel." Jenny busied herself with grabbing another slice of pizza while sending Abby a meaningful look that she wouldn't stay long.

A lull in the conversation ratcheted the tension in the room until Jenny burst the bubble. "I'm sorry. Sometimes I'm like a bull in a china shop. I love Abby and only want what's best for her. You two seem to have huge chemistry. I'm excited for her. I'm going to go now and leave you two to work out whatever it is you need to resolve." Jenny hugged Abby and whispered in her ear. "I have a good feeling about this one, don't let her get away."

***

After Jenny made her hasty retreat, the dead silence was punctuated with the loud purr from Plato. Abby continued to pet him more as a comfort to herself than as a way to dote on Plato.

Muse picked up another slice of pizza, ripping a chunk off the end almost savagely and then chewing slowly before declaring, "I like pizza."

There was so much more to explore than this declaration which suggested this was the first time Muse had ever eaten pizza. Her demeanor was stiff, and the strain was evident in her voice, along with a painted-on smile that definitely did not reach her eyes. No, her eyes held a kind of sadness that made Abby want to wrap her in a protective cocoon.

"Muse, talk to me. Something is terribly wrong, and I want to help."

"You can't."

"Why not?"

"You just can't. Leave it be, Abby, please," Muse pleaded. There was a kind of desperation in her voice that left Abby almost defeated. She did the only thing she could think of to do. She wrapped Muse in her arms and directed her head onto her shoulder. The wetness came almost instantaneously. Muse was crying. It wasn't like Abby had never comforted a crying woman, but somehow this felt different.

Muse lifted her head from Abby's shoulder and wiped her eyes. She'd missed a spot, and the tears clung to her cheek. "This is sadness, isn't it?"

"I don't know, Muse. Only you can define what you are feeling." Abby brushed away the remaining moisture.

"People cry when they are sad." Muse's innocent eyes lifted to Abby's for an answer.

"Not always. Haven't you ever heard of tears of joy?"

"I don't believe these are tears of joy."

"No, I don't expect they are. Your face is all wrong for that." Abby placed her hand against Muse's cheek to give her a reassuring caress.

"We should talk about sex now. Maybe that will cheer me up. I hear it's something to enjoy and celebrate."

Abby felt the abruptness of the declaration and wasn't sure how to interpret the detour. She pulled away to give herself enough distance. The proximity and closeness of their earlier exchange had gone. Nothing remained to mark the spot.

"Whoa. Muse, I can't have sex with you because I get the sense that you'll walk out of my life in a very short time and never return. I don't sleep with women I won't ever see again. That's not me. If you thought it was, you picked the wrong person." Her voice came out more harshly than she intended.

"We'll remain connected."

"What does that mean? You'll text me? Maybe even call? Will you pop in again? Make this your go-to vacation spot? Allow me to visit, wherever you land?" Abby felt her irritation rise, slowly, gathering speed like a hurricane off the coast in warm water.

"I want you to keep the motorcycle. I won't need it anymore."

Abby stood and took a few steps before remembering her toe. "Ow. Stop it, Muse. Answer my damn questions." Her voice rose as she turned to face Muse and glared at her.

"Anger. That is anger."

"You're damn right it is. Contrary to popular belief, I get angry like everyone else. I feel hurt, pain, anger, love. I'm capable of a lot of emotions."

"Me, too," Muse whispered.

Abby sucked in air and blew it out slowly, counting to ten in her head. "Will you please answer one of my questions? Will I ever see you again?"

"No. I'm sorry, Abby. As much as I would like that to happen, you have to know that I would. I can't…"

Exasperation found fuel, and the fire inside her ignited. "Why not?"

"I can't answer that. Please don't ask me to. Will you let me enjoy the scrap of time I have left on vacation with you? We can do anything you want. You don't have to indulge my whims."

"But that's just it. I want to indulge your whims. I want to keep on being the one to tease out your smile, your laugh, your joy." She kept a lid on her exasperation, not allowing the fire to blow out the windows.

"Perhaps I'll be permitted to explain at the close of my vacation. That's a compromise that surely my boss can live with."

Abby didn't like feeling this dread, so she did the only thing she knew to advance the conversation and remove the feeling. "Witness protection?" The joke earned a smile from Muse.

"Good guess, but no. Can we revisit the sex thing?" Muse joked back.

Abby's resolve started to wane. What was the harm? When would she ever have the chance with such a perfect woman? The ideal of beauty. Abby had honestly never seen a woman as stunning as Muse, not to mention interacted with one. She smiled, almost a smile of acceptance. Almost.

"How about we share the same bed tonight? Fully clothed. I would like to at least feel another body against my own. No sex. Just cuddling?" Hope edged Muse's voice as she floated the idea to Abby.

"Why do I believe this is a horrible idea that I'm going to agree to?"

Muse's face lit up, and that was all it took to persuade Abby. If she could generate that reaction, Abby wanted to comply with whatever suggestion Muse made. That smile might even be enough to get her to break her rigid rules around sex.

***

Muse's arm fell across Abby's belly, and she felt the soft warmth against her own stomach. She immensely enjoyed cuddling. She would definitely miss this when she went back. However, she wouldn't wish for the urgency that took over her body and required separation from Abby. Muse slipped carefully from the bed and shuffled into the bathroom. Urination was necessary, but did she have to feel the need in the middle of the night when she was so comfortable spooning Abby? Her light adorable snoring had lulled Muse to sleep before another sensation threatened to take over.

Rubbing her eyes, Muse let her bare bottom touch the cold porcelain. She was startled from her half-sleeping state by Calli's harsh tone.

"What the Hades are you thinking? Cuddling? You know that leads to sex."

"I certainly hope so." Muse grinned at her colleague, who stood with her arms crossed in a very human gesture of displeasure.

"You can't have sex with her. I forbid it."

"Death had sex with the woman he fell in love with. Why can't I? Besides, I don't believe you when you said it didn't work out for him. In two of the inspired stories, he took her back with him. Happy ending."

"You know very well that's different. Everyone ends up being snatched by Death. Death would have taken her, eventually. You can't bring Abby back with you, and you know it."

"I can stay here. I can inspire Abby in a different way." Muse propped her head in her hand and sighed. *That would be a fantasy come true*, she thought. As if suddenly woken from a dream, her head popped up, and she hissed, "What are you doing here? In Abby's bathroom? She's going to hear us."

"You should have thought of that before you started cuddling with her."

"What's got you so rattled? One of us choosing a different path shouldn't be such a big deal. Wait. You believe I'll start a movement. I heard a rumor that it happened before. Does the name Dumi ring a bell?"

Calli looked away, and Muse got the impression she was hiding something before gritting her teeth and whispering, "Don't you understand? Have you read Abby's social media posts? They are getting exponentially worse with every hour you spend on this unnecessary vacation of yours. Can't you comprehend how crucial we are to this world where you've fallen in love?"

"What if they could acquire their inspiration without us? I walked along the beach. Rode a motorcycle. Looked across a blue lake with only a hint of a ripple. Ate a piece of pizza! And snuggled against a beautiful woman. I feel inspired. Why shouldn't they? Maybe they don't need us. Perhaps it's the other way around. We need them to justify our existence."

"Preposterous. If you were following what is happening in your territory, you would know that."

"Okay, good point. But maybe we could perform our jobs more efficiently, and then you could divvy my territory to the others?"

"Muse?" Abby's sleepy voice called, and Muse knew she was out of bed and on the other side of the door.

She waved frantically at Calli and hissed, "Go, before she finds you."

A knock on the door was enough to entice Calli to leave. Muse knew their conversation was not finished, but at least it had given her additional food for thought. For the very first time, she considered remaining with Abby. That thought elicited an unusual feeling in her stomach. There was a kind of fluttering inside, and she couldn't help the goofy grin that appeared on her face. Could this be love?

"I'm fine, Abby. I believe I have a bladder the size of a pea." Muse was happy that she remembered that familiar phrase. Tugging on the end of the roll of toilet paper, she quickly wiped her private area, eager to return to the glorious feeling of holding a beautiful woman against her body. Even though they were both clothed, nothing had compared so far to the joy of that simple pleasure.

***

Abby had awakened in a great mood and decided to put on music using her portable Bluetooth speaker to connect seamlessly with her phone. Earlier, she had slipped from the bed, kissing Muse on the cheek and telling her it was too early to wake yet. Abby swayed to the music. She was careful not to put her full weight on her injured foot with the broken toe as she prepared a special meal for Muse. Slicing the first piece of French toast in the middle, Abby slathered one side with goat cheese and brought the two pieces together. Setting this one slice on the cookie sheet in the oven to warm, she felt a presence behind her. Abby didn't believe she imagined the extra bounce in Muse's step.

"Good morning. Coffee is on the counter. Help yourself." Abby gestured to the carafe of coffee. "I'm almost done here. I hope you'll like my special stuffed French toast."

"I'm sure I will. I have loved all the food you've introduced me to."

"How did you sleep?" Abby flipped a piece of toast in her frying pan and then glanced in Muse's direction to gauge her response.

Muse beamed. "Much better than the previous night when I did not have you in my arms. And you?"

Abby blushed. "Ditto."

"I've been thinking about the barriers to having sex with you, Abby. What if—"

"I'll do it," Abby blurted as she flipped the toast to a waiting plate, removed the frying pan from the hot burner, and turned to face Muse.

Muse set the coffee she had prepared onto the counter and approached Abby. Her hand brushed along the side of Abby's face. "Are you sure? I'm feeling something new, Abby. There's a flutter in my belly." She moved in and captured Abby's lips. Her tongue snaked lazily inside as Muse explored every inch of her mouth with tenderness. There was a hint of passion, but neither woman pushed further. As if there were an unspoken agreement, both continued to explore one another without ratcheting the intensity. The message hinted at having all the time in the world even though Abby knew reality might be the exact opposite.

Abby had to use the back of the counter for support. When they broke apart but remained mere inches from one another, Abby responded, "I have that fluttering, too."

"Now my knees seem like they will drag me to the ground. I might fall and become as clumsy as you."

Abby laughed and then playfully pushed Muse away. "Stop distracting me, or my agreement might result in both of us returning to bed right this second."

Muse pecked Abby on the lips once more before moving away. "Okay, but only because I want to taste this French toast you're making. There is something sweet-smelling in the air that tells me I'll like this breakfast."

"It's the cinnamon. That always tickles my olfactory glands. If it were up to me, I would require that every dessert has a bit of cinnamon, not to mention a few other dishes that might benefit from this wonderful spice. I'd give up garlic if I had to. The one spice I can never go without is cinnamon. I should make you my famous cinnamon rolls. Tomorrow," Abby absently added as she returned the frying pan to the burner and dipped another slice of thick toast into the batter.

"I see you're favoring one leg. Is your broken toe bothering you?" Muse asked.

"Nah, I'm used to navigating my kitchen and going about my business with minor injuries."

"So, cinnamon rolls tomorrow, yes, a possible turning point deserves baked goods."

Abby was not going to ruminate about yet another cryptic statement by Muse when she felt such exuberance.

***

As the women were about to leave for their long drive to the lake, picnic basket in hand, Abby's phone rang. She looked at the screen and sighed before swiping it to answer. "Hello…Yes, we aren't going to back out…Okay, tell me what you're serving, and I'll bring an appropriate bottle or two that will pair well with the meal…Shut up, I know what wines go with what, and even if I don't, I can Google it. Google is my friend, you know. Many of life's most interesting mysteries have been solved by a simple Google…Yeah, yeah, see you around six. Bye, Jenno."

Muse studied Abby as she talked with Jenny. She tried to figure out how Abby felt about going to dinner with Jenny and her new love interest. She decided it was best to ask. "Are you really okay with going to dinner at Jenny's tonight? Or are you being polite and doing what is expected of you?"

Abby shrugged. "Probably a little of both."

"Do you still love her?" Muse held her breath as Abby formulated her reply.

Using her free hand, Abby limped to the couch, dragging Muse with her. Muse noted this seemed to be the place where they had their most serious discussions. Setting the picnic basket to the side and facing Muse, Abby began.

"Of course I still love her. She's my best friend, and that won't change because the way I loved her was different from the way she loves me."

"The way you loved her, as in past tense?" Muse raised her eyebrow. "Was that a slip of the tongue?" She smiled.

Abby paused, and her face scrunched in confusion. "I said, 'loved'?"

"You did."

"Hmm. I need to think about this a bit more. To be honest, my emotions are jumbled right now. I can't pinpoint them. What I know is that I don't believe it will hurt as much to see them together as it might have a few months ago when I was still raw. It was good of Nat to call. I missed hanging with Jenny. She can be brash and pushy, but Jenny truly has a heart of gold."

"I think I see that. I misbehaved yesterday. I should apologize to Jenny."

"She'll get over it. Jenny doesn't hold grudges. At all. I, on the other hand, have been known to be rather stubborn. I don't think I would have reached out to her if Nat hadn't called. My pride was so bruised I couldn't see what was right in front of my face. I knew deep inside that Jenny never had those kinds of feelings for me. Wanting them to surface after all those years without the slightest hint they were simmering below was a cruel fantasy that I, and I alone, interjected into the equation."

"I don't think you manufactured the affection she has for you. I think you concocted a specific type of affection."

"Yeah, you hit the nail squarely on the head. See, that's why I never wield a hammer. It doesn't end well. Neither literally nor figuratively. I need to have more direct communication, more often if I want to know the answers to the mysteries of the universe or that slippery little bugger, love."

"What kind of affection do you feel for me?" Muse asked.

"You can't tell?"

"I'm still new to these experiences. I think I need a guide."

"The kind of affection that leads to sex," Abby answered, while pulling Muse to her feet. "Now come on, I promised you a romantic picnic lunch at the lake, and by golly, that is exactly what we'll have."

CHAPTER NINE

A few wispy clouds traveled idly across the otherwise clear blue sky. As the sun moved higher, the increasing warmth of the day heated Abby's body, making her heavy sweatshirt too much. She yanked off the unnecessary layer and pulled out her T-shirt to air-dry the sweat that had formed on her skin. Then she lay back on the blanket Muse had unfolded earlier.

"What a beautiful day. I've been such a troll lately. Whining about my writer's block and everything else in my life that isn't going exactly the way I want, while here I am, living in one of the most gorgeous places on this planet. I have food, a roof over my head, enough money in the bank to live out my life—maybe not in luxury, but still. I'm an ungrateful bitch."

"What would you do if your writer's block never went away?" Muse asked, lowering herself to the blanket to lie beside Abby.

Abby moved her hands behind her head and clasped them together. "I don't know. Being a writer has defined me for the last fifteen years. Honestly, I think I would feel lost, floating uncomfortably in this so-called life I've carved out for myself. I'm not sure I could survive that. I'd feel like a complete and utter failure at the one thing I've been good at, or moderately good at."

"I'm sure that's not true. Certainly, you're proficient at many things. You're good at entertaining me. You're an accomplished cook. I'm hoping you are skillful at sex." Muse turned on her side and grinned.

Abby met Muse's smiling face and propped her head on her hand. "I'll bet you're a top-notch editor. But you probably don't have to be good at anything with your stunning looks."

"What if this is merely an outer covering and not something that defines me?" Muse sighed.

"A mighty fine outer covering if you ask me." When Abby hazarded a glance in Muse's direction, the sadness in her eyes caused Abby to add, "You are not merely your outer covering. You've got this kindness and innocence about you that's hard to resist. You make a person feel instantly at ease, so thoroughly that I invited you to stay with me, and I didn't know a single thing about you. That is a gift. And another thing, your name fits you. You inspire me to be a better person. I'm inclined to consider stepping out of my rut, to enjoy life and everything around me that holds beauty. That's your superpower."

"What if you had to choose between love and purpose? Which would you choose?" Muse asked.

"I don't know. Love sounds amazing." Abby couldn't help the wistfulness in her voice. "Who would be harmed if I never wrote another book for the rest of my life? No loss, really." She closed her eyes for a moment.

"Your readers would lose a great deal."

"I don't think so, but if I were completely honest, even if I never sold another book for the rest of my life, I would miss writing. I guess it's in my blood. I'd have to wonder if the price of true love is too high if I had to give up writing."

"Do you think that people only have one purpose in life? What about those star athletes who have an injury and their career is suddenly gone? They find another purpose," Muse argued. "I've heard people change careers an average of twelve to fifteen times in their lifetime. Surely that means there is not just one purpose."

"Maybe, but I'll bet it isn't careers but jobs. That's a completely different thing. Also, summer jobs, or stuff you do while going to college, don't count." Abby paused and shrugged.

"I've only had one job, one purpose."

"Seriously? I think a job or even a career and a purpose are completely different things. That's cool that yours match up. Gosh, I've been everything from a dishwasher to a telemarketer. Nothing felt right until I started writing." Abby brushed to the side a lock of hair that had fallen over her eyes. "Making money at it was the absolute cherry on the top. But that isn't why I'm so bothered by my block. It isn't about the money. It's about this bottled up feeling. Like I'm constipated, and I know that's not healthy. I could try an enema, but that might mean a bunch of diarrhea on the page. Not good. Or I could try to dig it out. Equally gross."

Muse laughed. "Your analogies are…"

"I know. Sometimes I can't help myself. That's why my writing is an acquired taste for many. Good thing there are enough people who like odd. It's getting late. We should probably head back, so we have enough time to get ready and pick up wine. Copious amounts of wine. You're driving, and I'm drinking."

"I don't drive anywhere. It's probably not a good idea to have me drive. Cars aren't necessary where I'm from." Muse began packing the remnants of their lunch.

Abby stood and stretched while putting her weight once again on her uninjured foot. "Ah, another clue. Big city? Ubers everywhere, huh? Or do you take the bus?"

"Something like that." Each woman took a corner of the blanket and began folding it until they met in the center and giggled before they kissed.

***

The moment the click of the lock turned and Abby opened her front door, Plato rushed to greet the two women. Muse was delighted that, finally, Abby's cat was warming to her. She thought that was a direct reflection on how comfortable she felt weaving herself into Abby's world and life. He had curled at the bottom of the bed the previous evening but continued to keep his distance. Muse decided to take a chance and squatted to run her hand along his fur. Even though his silky hair looked soft, as soft as Abby's hair, Muse was surprised by the texture. She liked the sensation on her hand as she petted him, and his response was a rumbling that appeared to bubble from his throat.

"You've finally received the stamp of approval from Plato. Let me tell you, that's not an easy thing to accomplish. One or two of my past girlfriends never reached that pinnacle."

"Girlfriends?" Muse arched her eyebrow. "As in plural?"

"I'm not a nun or a hermit. I have dated before. Is that so hard to believe? I haven't spent my entire adult life pining after Jenny."

"Do we have time to sit before getting ready for dinner?" Muse reluctantly stopped petting Plato and stood waiting for direction from Abby.

"Sure, come on." Abby limped to the couch while Muse followed. "I have a hunch I'm about to be grilled on my past lovers."

"Oh, yes. I would like to hear all about them." Muse clapped her hands once in excitement.

"I don't know if I like talking about them. Next to you and your, uh, apparent lack of experience, I feel like a floozy."

"Oh, no. I am not judging. I'm jealous. My circumstances are so different. I was never afforded the same opportunities before I demanded a vacation. If you have had so many lovers, why are you not paired with one of them?"

Abby scratched her head. "Good question. Writers aren't the easiest people to live with. When I would get an inspiration, I'd stop whatever I was doing, no matter what that was, and grab any scrap of paper near me to jot things down. The compulsion was so strong it was hard to describe. I suppose that made me the kind of person who was never totally present with someone else. Then, there is the fact that no one matches up with the characters in my novels, whom I sort of fall in love with when I write them. They aren't perfect, but their flaws are. Or at least their imperfections are hard to resist."

"You've been completely present with me. I feel like all of your focus is right here." Muse touched her heart.

"Well, sure. I'm still in the midst of a huge writer's block. There's nowhere else for my energy to go. It's not that I'm incapable of giving someone my undivided attention, but

I can only do this intermittently." Abby leaned back against the couch cushions.

"Doesn't life present numerous distractions? Surely writers or artists are not the only people inconsistent with their affections."

"True, but I believe writers excel at it."

"How many lovers had you had?" Muse was very interested in the answer to this question.

"Four." The response came in a breath of hesitation, and Muse wondered if Abby was embarrassed by the number. Was it unusually large or small in Abby's estimation?

Taking what she thought was the safe path, Muse asked, "Will you tell me about them?" She didn't want to make Abby feel ashamed about her number.

"Not much to tell. My exes are perfectly lovely women. Nothing terribly unique. After the initial excitement, the feelings weren't strong enough to make it through the tough times. I'm not blaming any of them. All the break-ups were mutual."

"You sound so matter of fact about something as important as love."

"Don't get me wrong, whenever something ends, there is always pain, but there was never enough love to work through the hard times. If I were honest, I knew that right from the start in every situation and simply took the ride until the eventual conclusion. I'm cautious now and don't jump in with both feet anymore. I used to be a lot more spontaneous with my assertions of love. I suppose that's why it's still a bit raw with Jenny. I deliberately delayed making the declaration. It took years for me to accept my feelings for her. I don't know how I completely missed the cues regarding how she felt about me." Abby shook her head.

"One thing I have missed is the closeness of having someone next to me at night. I realized that last night. That simple touch that I used to count on whenever I was in a relationship. I want that with someone whom I'll care enough about to endure the rough spots."

"I'll miss that too." Muse looked away.

"I wish you would open up to me." Abby used her hand to turn Muse's face.

"We should get ready. I'll take a shower after you're finished."

Abby took both of Muse's hands into her own and requested a promise. "Before you leave tomorrow, I want to know where you live and make sure that whatever you're going to is safe. I can't let you leave without discovering that."

"Okay."

With that simple acknowledgment and victory won, Abby leaned in and sealed the deal with a kiss.

***

After Abby had half-skipped, half-limped into the bathroom, clearly overjoyed by what Muse had agreed to, Muse buried her head in her hands.

"What have I done?"

"Yes, what have you done? You know, Muse, you're adopting their gestures now. What's next?" Calli leaned casually against the wall in the living room.

"Calli, you're like an overprotective mother or overly critical grandmother." Muse rolled her eyes.

"Really?" Calli raised her eyebrow and then looked away again. There was definitely something she was hiding. *Interesting.*

"Calli, you can't continue to pop in like this. You're the one who keeps warning me. What if she sees you?"

"How will that matter if you tell her who you really are?" Calli pushed away from the wall and waved her hand as if swatting a fly. "Besides, can't you hear the water running? We have a few more minutes before she exits the shower."

"Fine. Go ahead and lecture me. Get it over with and then vamoose."

"Vamoose? What the hell is that?"

"It means go away. For good."

"Okay, here is some new advice. Have sex with Abby. Expunge it from your system, and then we can move past this temporary detour. At least you won't produce a child if you have sex. While you've been gone, your work has piled up, and you'll be busy for half an eternity catching up."

"Why can't the rest of you pick up the slack? Why do I have to return to a mess? Wait, what? You're actually telling me to have sex with Abby?" Muse stared at Calli, trying to determine if what she'd just said was genuine acceptance.

Calli shrugged. "Yeah, but on one condition. You know you can't tell her about us. The consequences would be disastrous. You can't be that selfish."

"What consequences?"

"The delicate balance between inspiration and art. You, more than anyone, recognize how that balance is sometimes affected by the slightest event. You won't simply be failing with one artist. You could affect an entire territory."

"Hasn't Zeus ever replaced one of us?"

"I am not answering that question. It will only feed those rumors that you seem to believe run rampant among our colleagues. I know that your audacity in demanding a bloody vacation is a first, and look where that's gotten us. You know this region is in a panic right now?"

"Oh, please. You're so theatrical. I'll bet you've inspired your subjects to be overly dramatic. No wonder that part of the world is known for telenovelas."

"Hey, don't forget Latin music. Come on, you can't beat, get it, 'beat,' pun intended, music that begs a person to sway their hips and dance with abandon."

"True," Muse reluctantly answered. "I don't believe you about the consequences. She deserves to know the truth, and I agreed. It's done. She won't believe me anyway, and maybe it will inspire her to write a new novel. I'll have given her the idea. It's a win-win."

Calli's head jerked up, and Muse heard the absence of water running.

"Please, Muse, think about it before you jump headfirst into a pool without any water. Don't forget his warnings because you've fallen head over heels in love. It doesn't mean you have to act so irresponsibly. Hanging with the subjects has somehow injected a kind of virus into you. Now you're thinking, talking, and feeling like one of them. And that is not good. No, not at all good."

Muse made a go away motion with her hands and hissed, "Disappear. Please, before she sees you."

The bathroom door creaked open, and Abby poked her head out. "Muse, who are you talking to?"

"No one. Stop hogging the bathroom." Like a charm, the redirection worked as the door closed, and then Abby emerged wearing a bathrobe.

"Bossy much?" Abby chuckled. "It's all yours." She swept from the room dramatically.

Muse hurried into the bedroom and grabbed the saddlebag with her extra set of clothes. Slipping past Abby, she shot her a weak smile before closing the bathroom door and resting her head against the door for a minute. "Damn," she muttered, and then proceeded to strip off her clothes and turn on the shower. The warm water cascaded over her body, finally allowing her to relax. She only had one more night with Abby, and she was determined to make the best of it. Maybe agreeing to dinner hadn't been such a grand idea after all. That would mean less alone time with Abby. The sands were flowing too quickly in the hourglass.

***

When Jenny opened the door, Abby couldn't help but notice the tall man standing close behind her with a broad smile on his face. He was attractive enough, even with his close-cropped hair intended to mask his balding head. Some men could wear their baldness well and be considered sexy. Abby decided David fell into that category. He had a strong jaw, full lips, and large gray eyes set inside a pair of eyelashes a woman would kill for. Clearly, David engaged in regular exercise and maybe lifted weights, considering his broad shoulders, trim waistline, and defined muscles in the visible areas.

Abby held up two bottles of wine and pointed to Muse, who carried their additional bounty. "We've brought four different wines, so I suspect we have definitely covered all our bases to be sure to match whatever you've prepared.

Although, I'll bet my car it's grilled chicken, asparagus, a beautiful salad, and maybe roasted red potatoes."

"Fine, be a smartass," Jenny said.

"It's your go-to meal for whenever you have company. I am your best friend. I should know these facts."

Jenny smiled and shook her head. She pointed at David. "Muse, Abby, this is David. David, meet my best friend, Abby." Jenny waved her hand in Abby's direction. "And, her lovely, uh, companion, Muse."

Jenny grabbed the bottles from Muse and glanced at the labels. "Nice. David, grab the other two from Abby. We're going to have ourselves a party tonight."

If possible, David's smile grew wider as he took the bottles from Abby. "I'm so happy you could come to dinner."

"Okay." Abby limped as she followed Jenny into the kitchen and whispered in her ear, "Um, I'll admit, he's easy on the eyes, but uh, is he a little slow? Not that it's a bad thing. I suppose conventional intelligence isn't always the most important trait to have."

"Shush, you'll know soon enough," Jenny responded in a low voice. She set down her two bottles on the counter and turned to her new love interest. "David, honey, will you choose one of these wines and open the bottle for us while we settle into the living room? We have time before dinner is ready."

"Sure thing, hon," David answered with enthusiasm. He was still staring at Abby like she was a piece of prime rib after being denied red meat for years.

"Why is he staring at me? It's creepy," Abby mumbled as Jenny led Muse and Abby to the other room.

Ignoring Abby's observation, Jenny said, "I see you did a number to that toe of yours. You're limping again."

Abby shrugged. "Minor injury. Although I think I have a record going. I'm dealing with three at the moment. Tailbone, toe, and head." She pointed to the tiny line on her forehead.

Abby had always loved Jenny's house. She had a great eye and had accented the solid wood floors and handcrafted stone fireplace perfectly with the soft moss-colored couch and muted tones in the rug covering over half of the floor, leaving the wood to peek from the perimeter. Muse sat on the sofa and looked around, smiling as she took in her surroundings. Abby joined her on the larger sitting option while Jenny opted for the love seat.

"I'm so happy to bring my favorite two people together, finally. No offense, Muse. I don't know you that well to include you in that declaration. My daughter doesn't count either. She's more like my sweet little apple blossom. I'm speaking strictly adult persons."

Not more than a minute later, David entered carrying wine glasses. He handed them to Muse and Abby, then hurried back with two more glasses that he retrieved from the kitchen. David sat next to Jenny and casually rested his hand on her knee.

"What shall we toast to? New love?" Jenny asked.

Abby nearly spilled her wine as she met her best friend's eyes and her cheeky wink, but managed to clink the other glasses. Muse tentatively touched her wine glass with all the others and watched everyone take a sip before bringing the glass to her lips.

"I can't tell you how excited I am to meet you," David gushed.

"Okay, let's settle this right now. I don't do kink. We are not going to have a threesome or foursome, so knock that shit right out of your head."

"What? No, no, I, uh, I would never," David stuttered.

"Really, Abby? Is that what you think?" Jenny shook her head in disbelief.

"I'm assuming you told him that I'm a lesbian."

"I didn't have to. David is a huge fan of your books and has read your biography. I think he loves you so much he cyberstalked you."

"Yeah, I love thrillers, and you weave the best stories. The twists are brilliant. I, uh, kind of tried to write a medical thriller. I'd love it if you could read it and tell me what you think."

"Oh, uh, I'm sorry." Abby blushed.

David continued to grin like a madman until he abruptly popped from the couch and sprinted down the hallway toward Jenny's bedroom. Abby quirked her eyebrow at Jenny. "Okay, enough already. You don't have to make your boyfriend fawn over me to get me to like him."

"I'm not, honest, Abby." Jenny laughed.

David returned to the living room with a stack of books in his hands. "I would have brought them all, but Jenny told me not to. She said we would have plenty of time to hang out, and I shouldn't overwhelm you. Do you think you can sign these for me?" He sounded so genuinely excited. Abby was indeed warming to his boyish exuberance. She didn't believe she'd ever seen a middle-aged man do the fangirl thing. Was there such a thing as a fanboy?

Abby laughed and extended her hand for the first book. "Good choice. I know writers aren't supposed to have favorite babies, but this one is mine for sure," she stage-whispered while cupping her free hand against her mouth. "Um, Jenny, do you have a pen I can borrow?"

David pulled a pen from his pocket and presented it to Abby like it was an engagement ring. The silly grin on his face remained. "Here, you can use this one."

"A boy scout, huh? Always prepared," Abby joked before starting to scribble a short personal message on the first book.

"Okay, David, you can take it down a notch or two. I'm starting to get jealous, and I know Abby wouldn't give you the time of day. She's strictly into woman parts."

"I know," he scoffed. "I can admire women for reasons other than wanting to date them."

Muse remained quiet while the whole uncomfortable interaction occurred until stating softly, "I understand his infatuation. She's really something." Muse met Abby's eyes, and Abby stopped breathing for a second. No woman had ever looked at her like that before.

After Abby set the first book on the table, David handed her another. "So, Abby, are you still in a writer's block, too?"

"Huh?" Abby looked up from the book she'd just inscribed.

"Yeah, it's like this massive news story right now," David added.

"What is?" Muse asked.

"There are reports from painters, sculptors, musicians, and writers all around the Pacific Northwest describing this weird sort of absence of inspiration. I've read about this psychological phenomenon called mass hysteria. At first, I chalked it up to that, but the tales are eerily familiar. Then, when Jenny told me you've been blocked for months and it didn't happen a couple of days ago like all the rest, it got me to wondering."

"Wow, freaky." Abby paused and set the pen down, glancing in Muse's direction. She wasn't sure why she was looking at Muse. Maybe for support or reassurance. It was odd. Muse had turned white, and suddenly Abby was petrified. She didn't know what exactly scared her, and that was even more puzzling.

"What else are the news people saying?" Muse's wobbled question emerged with what Abby thought was a great deal of trepidation.

"Oh, you know how the news can present everything in an overly dramatic fashion. End of cultured civilization, beauty, and emotion as we know it. I mean, I'm certainly appreciative of the arts. I love Abby's books, but the end of cultured civilization and love?"

"Love? Why the end of love?" Abby leaned forward. She couldn't see how love and art were connected.

"Because art inspires the deepest of emotions, and the pinnacle of those emotions is love. It's what makes the world go round, and art is what spins that world. Art inspires action, too. Can you imagine a world without music, books, plays, paintings, photography? The blandness might be the end of civilization as we know it. But I can't imagine this weird blip meaning the end of art. Besides, it's only happening in Washington, Oregon, and Idaho. Odd, huh?" David grinned and handed her another book as if what they were talking about were daily mundane news.

Abby started inscribing the next book. "Well, I don't own a TV, so I haven't heard any of this news. I did notice an uptick in the social media comments about writer's block. I thought it was a weird fluke, and I was simply noticing because of my personal situation. I had no idea this bizarre phenomenon extended beyond writing."

"I should probably check on the chicken. Are you guys hungry?" Jenny asked.

"I am." Abby looked expectantly at Muse, anticipating that she would chime in.

Muse stared straight ahead as if she saw a ghost. An evil ghost. Abby didn't care one bit about Muse's uncharacteristic quietness in light of Jenny's questioning looks. Jenny and David's impression of Muse wasn't the problem. The issue was that Muse was not her cheerful self.

While Jenny pulled the chicken from the grill, David attempted to get to know Muse, asking, "So, Muse, how did you and Abby meet?"

"On the beach." Muse's answer was clipped, offering no further details.

Abby jumped in to fill in the specifics. "I face-planted right in front of her as she walked on the beach. After I learned she was on vacation, I offered to be her own personal tour guide." Abby smiled at Muse but didn't get any reaction.

The awkward silence was disrupted by Jenny's return as she carried the grilled chicken on a platter, adding it to the other covered dishes already on the table. "Grub's up. Come on, time to eat."

Everyone took their seats at the table, mumbling words of appreciation as Jenny began to pass around the serving plates and bowls.

Between forkfuls of food, David made another attempt to engage Muse. "Muse, are you also a fan of Abby's books?"

"Yes, of course." Once again, she kept her response short, offering only a brief glance in his direction.

Abby noticed how pale Muse looked and leaned in to ask, "Are you feeling okay?"

Muse nodded. Her fork chased around the food that rarely made it into her mouth.

David glanced at Jenny with a wrinkled forehead. Jenny raised her eyebrow at Abby but chose to redirect the conversation, ignoring the change that started as a fun evening but quickly devolved.

"Abby, when is your new book coming out?" Jenny asked.

"Yes, I would love to know the answer to that," David added. "I'm eagerly anticipating a new installment."

The evening continued in the same painful vein. Muse's inquisitiveness that Abby had learned to appreciate disappeared into awkward silences, leaving the bulk of the evening to David and Jenny, who directed the remainder of their questions to Abby. Although Abby wasn't usually the kind of person to fill in the gaps, she asked David about his work and tried to catch up with what she'd missed in Jenny's life.

When Jenny removed the dishes from the table, most of the food remained on Muse's plate. With the table cleared and the evening's increased clumsiness, Abby decided to offer a humane ending to the night by making a weak excuse for leaving early.

"Um, I think I left Plato outside, and he'll probably be ready to give me a long lecture if we don't head back." Abby stood, wiping her sweaty hands on her pants.

Walking Muse and Abby to the door, Jenny pulled Abby to the side and, while hugging her, asked, "Did David cause your girlfriend to clam up? What the hell happened? She was so…I don't know, lively when I met her at Pacific Pizza."

"I'm as perplexed as you are. I'll talk to you later after I've had a chance to figure it out. I promise. And she's not exactly my girlfriend. I don't know if I'll see her again after she leaves tomorrow."

"Oh." Jenny sounded disappointed. Abby suspected Jenny wanted Abby to have what she and David clearly had. They were in that googly eyes stage. After the initial shine of meeting Abby wore off, David's attention boomeranged to Jenny, and he only had eyes for her during dinner.

"I like him," Abby declared. Although her voice held a certain amount of hesitation, she was confident in her assessment of him. She'd seen that look before, and if she truly loved her best friend, she needed to get over herself and be happy for the couple.

"Do you honestly?" Jenny asked.

Abby nodded.

"You have no idea how happy I am about that. I was so worried. So, we're okay?"

"Yeah, we're fine. You're my best friend. You'll always be my best friend. I think I was more in love with the notion of us being together than the reality. You would have driven me crazy."

Jenny smacked Abby on the arm. "Thanks, thanks a lot. Hey, don't give up on the mute one. I definitely saw something before."

"Thank you for dinner," Abby said.

"Yeah, thanks," Muse murmured as she stood awkwardly, several feet away.

Muse seemed to recognize the need to give Jenny and Abby space at the close of the evening. Abby thought about how she couldn't afford that luxury with Muse. If she had to pry out what the hell was going on with a very large crowbar, she would. One more evening and Muse had promised.

David called from the kitchen, where he was finishing the dishes, "Hey, next time, I'll bring the rest of my collection of books for you to sign."

Jenny laughed. "I know, I know. He's a bit of a dork, but sweet. Very sweet."

"I'll bring my pen," Abby called back. "See ya later. I'll call you tomorrow."

***

By the time Abby and Muse hit the road, everything was shrouded in darkness. Abby squinted through her dirty windshield when the headlights of oncoming vehicles shined through and partially blinded her. Driving at night was not one of her favorite activities, and she would usually avoid it at all costs, choosing to either remain at home or crash at Jenny's house. That was definitely not an option tonight.

Abby had opened and promptly closed her mouth several times, hoping to start a conversation. No words would come yet. Besides, she wanted to see Muse's reaction to her questions. She needed to see her eyes. Her mouth. Would her lips remain in the frozen straight line or curve upwards in the same manner Abby had become accustomed to over the past few days when Muse delighted in a new experience?

Venturing a side glance, Abby saw Muse's head turned toward the glass as she seemed to stare outside at the passing greenery that wasn't visible in the inky black darkness. The trip was painful on so many levels. This was not the comfortable silence of two people who knew each other well or connected immediately. Abby could not do a thing as that instant ease and attraction slipped away like sand through her fingers.

Without saying a single word, Abby tossed the keys on the counter with more force than she intended. She pointed to the couch and directed, "Sit. We're going to talk about what the hell happened at Jenny's. That was not jealousy. You promised full disclosure before we left, so out with it and include an explanation of tonight, please."

Muse looked like she was heading to the gallows as she slowly made her way to the couch. Sighing, she sat heavily.

Abby removed her jacket and tossed it on the chair adjacent to the couch. Sitting on the couch next to Muse, and turning to face her with an expectant look, she grabbed her hands.

Muse sighed. "I've been struggling with a decision. I almost made the wrong one, but tonight it became clear I only have one option."

Abby rolled her eyes. "Can you for once be a trifling less obtuse?"

"It's my fault what is happening with art. My selfish decision to take a vacation."

"You aren't making sense."

Muse sat a little straighter and declared with a fair amount of force in her voice. "I am Inspiration Northwest, Abby."

"What do you mean?"

"The reason inspired art came to a screeching halt in the Northwest is because I was burned out. It started with you, Abby. Every week a new subject lost their way, but three months ago, you started having a writer's block, and" — Muse pulled her hand away and pointed to her chest—

"nothing I tried altered that." Muse's hand dropped limply to her lap.

"You aren't to blame for my block. That's ridiculous. So much is happening in the writing world, and I don't know if I can compete or keep up with the changes. It's an evolution I wasn't prepared for. This is on me. I'm my own worst enemy." Abby grabbed her hand again, moving her fingers lightly across Muse's skin.

"Have you ever seen the old classic movie *Death Takes a Holiday*?" Muse asked.

"I have. And all the updated versions that came after. I loved that movie and the whole concept of Death taking a human form."

"A colleague of mine inspired one of her Italian subjects to write a play based on events that, in fact, did occur. Of course, the playwriter and filmmakers took poetic license, so all three versions are slightly different. My mentor insists it did not end well for Death, but I don't believe she knows what occurred."

"Look, if you don't want to tell me where you live, I'll accept that. I…I…have strong feelings for you, and I thought that maybe…but I don't seem to be able to read any situation lately. First, Jenny, and now you…"

"I've been wracking my brain to find a way, Abby. You haven't read the situation wrong. I was warned not to get involved. That has proved more difficult than I thought. I believe that ship has sailed, but I don't know if I broke the rule. He didn't exactly define involvement. Calli said we could have sex, but now I don't know if that's what he meant. Sometimes sex does not mean involvement, and sometimes it does. I'm so confused."

"He? He who? And who is Calli?"

"Zeus. How do I explain this in a way you'll understand?" Muse grabbed her chin in deep thought. "I suppose Zeus is there to direct us. To ensure inspiration continues to exist. In your world, I guess he would be my boss, and Calli would be my colleague. Calli is responsible for Mexico. I guess you could say she was my mentor. Similar to Death, we are the physical manifestation of Inspiration."

Abby blinked rapidly as her breathing increased. "You aren't making this up, are you?" Of all the confessions Abby had filtered through her brain, this was not one of them.

Muse bowed her head. "No, I'm not. I was told not to reveal myself unless absolutely necessary. I could only tell one person. I'm also forbidden from lying." Muse looked up and seemed to seek assurance from Abby. "Do you think allowing you to believe something was true when it was not is a lie? A lie by omission?"

"That is a huge debate. Sorry, for me personally, I believe when someone purposefully keeps a big secret and doesn't correct a wrong assumption, yeah, that's a lie. But others don't agree. I suppose it's open to interpretation. I don't know your boss, so I don't know what he's thinking. Maybe Calli can shed light on the matter. A mentor is supposed to do that."

"Calli is a pain in my rear, but I guess I should ask."

"What happens if you break the rules?"

"Zeus won't take me back," she stated as if that was obvious.

Abby smiled. "Is that such a bad thing? You could stay here…with me…" Abby felt a surge of hope.

"What about all the artists in the Pacific Northwest? I'll be abandoning them. Didn't you hear David? I would be the cause of the end of civilization and love. I can't be responsible for that." Muse wrung her hands together.

Abby tried to calm the situation by asking logical questions. "Don't you have a succession plan?"

"What is that?" Muse's body seemed to relax as she adopted a quizzical expression.

"Someone to take over for people when they leave an organization or retire."

"Inspiration doesn't leave or retire. We aren't structured like that." Her lips formed a grim line of reality.

"None of you have ever left? You said you had a mentor. There had to be a beginning. An orientation of sorts. If that happened with you, surely it can happen again with someone else."

Muse scratched her head and wrinkled her nose. "There are rumors. One of my sisters swears that happened eons ago. She won't tell me anything more about it, and neither will Calli. They were prepared. Art was not as prolific as it is today. There wasn't a need for as many of us. Somehow, Zeus knew and was able to forecast the increased demand. We were brought onboard in a planned fashion as growth occurred. There was a need to split the territories from few to many. They can't simply plop someone into the Northwest territory and be done with it. People will suffer. They already are."

Abby put her arm around Muse. "Don't worry, we'll figure it out. I'm a writer. I create loopholes all the time. We'll find one of those for this dilemma." Leaning in to kiss Muse seemed like the most natural thing to do. "Muse, I can't have sex with you."

"I understand." Muse's eyes began to water.

"No, I don't think you do. You didn't let me finish. We can't have sex, but we can make love. It won't be purely physical for me. Maybe it will be for you, but not for me. It won't be sex."

"I don't know exactly what Zeus meant by not getting involved, but I'm pretty sure making love would fit the definition. You know what? I don't care, because if what you're saying is correct, and I already broke the lie rule, it's a moot point. Another broken rule won't make it worse." Muse's brilliant smile returned to her face, and Abby felt such an explosion of emotion she pulled Muse to a standing position and led her to the bedroom. She had no intention of squandering what might be their last night together. Selfishly, she hoped that Muse had broken at least one rule. They could deal with the consequences later.

***

Muse wondered why her hands began to shake when Abby lifted her shirt over her head. Things were happening to her body that were so foreign she didn't know how to evaluate what was occurring. The tips of Abby's fingers floated over Muse's arms, making their way to her back. A wisp of air flowed over Muse's breasts the second Abby unhooked her bra. Now Muse's body began to shiver and lightly shake when the bra fell to the ground, and Abby moved her hand over Muse's breasts.

Muse wasn't sure what to do. She had never had this experience before, so she didn't know if she should be helping Abby remove her clothes. The sensation of brushing her own fingers across Abby's skin was too tempting to resist. Her hands quivered before landing on Abby's waist.

Curling her finger under Abby's loose shirt, Muse began to move the soft cotton inch by inch. Abby responded by removing her own hand that had just been caressing Muse's breast and lifted her arms in the air. With the shirt tossed to the side, Muse cautiously pushed Abby's bra straps down. However, the clasp was more challenging to undo than she had anticipated. She fumbled so inadequately with her shaking hands that Abby took pity on her and reached behind to assist Muse with her awkward first attempt to remove her bra.

"It's okay." Abby's warm smile was a balm to her nervousness. "Bras can be tricky."

"Breasts are very appealing to look at."

"And touch." Abby moved her hand back to Muse's breast and began to circle her nipple, very slowly.

"I would like to touch your breasts. May I?"

Abby nodded.

The two women stood half-naked, facing each other as Muse followed Abby's lead. She marveled at how smooth and soft Abby's breasts were. When her nipple began to pucker, she wondered if this was a positive reaction. Her own breasts mirrored the response, and the sensations were very welcome. Muse decided this was a good thing. If this simple touch generated such a powerful feeling, Muse was desperate to remove the remainder of their clothing and feel Abby's hands or mouth on the rest of her body. She'd read the descriptions in her subjects' books, and she was eager to explore those same sensations. Nothing short of a firsthand knowledge would do.

"I want to lie together unclothed. Can we do that?"

Abby grinned. "I certainly hope so. I could try to be all suave, but maybe it would be best if I remove my own pants." She chuckled. "I trust you can handle removing yours without my assistance."

Muse was so eager she felt like she was about to burst. "If it will get us closer to our naked bodies coming together, I wholeheartedly concur."

After both women had removed their clothing and climbed into Abby's bed, Abby didn't appear to be in any hurry as she ran her hands over Muse's body. When Abby moved close and began kissing Muse's neck and traveled down to her breasts, Muse began to squirm. She enjoyed the weight and the tingle she felt of skin on skin. Abby repositioned her body to capture Muse's mouth, rocking on top. Muse lost all rational thought and moved with Abby. The sensation intensified, and only one reflection remained. Muse did not want to leave Abby. She needed more time. She needed more of this. Abby's hand somehow found its way to the center of where the euphoria was mounting. Muse settled her hands on Abby's behind and held on.

Abby stopped kissing Muse long enough to ask, "Is this okay?"

"Oh, yes, Abby. I think I'm coming close to an orgasm. I don't know because I didn't do a practice run the first night on myself, but from the descriptions in the books…"

Abby laughed. "Stop analyzing and simply enjoy the experience."

"Okay."

Abby's fingertips slid over a sensitive spot, and Muse jerked. Abby immediately adjusted and eased around the tight curls and toward her opening, but never again directly in the exact area. She lingered around the same place several times as the wetness increased. Every so often, her fingers brushed lightly over that ultra-reactive tip, and Muse kept moving her body so Abby's fingers would connect again and again with where she felt that jolt of pleasure.

All these new sensations were almost too much for Muse, and every time Abby's fingers brushed closer to her opening, Muse had an overwhelming need for Abby to fill her by plunging inside.

"I want something else." Muse's voice surfaced in a breathy whisper.

"Tell me."

"Your fingers. Inside, please."

Abby pushed one, then two fingers inside, and still managed to use her thumb to reach the glorious bundle of nerves at the top. As the feelings heightened, so did Muse's emotions. She understood how this encounter was called making love. Even though this experience was brand new to her, Muse believed she'd fallen in love with Abby, and as the crescendo of physical sensation mounted, her only thought was this ultimate connection. She'd managed to push aside the fact that tomorrow, she'd be separating from Abby's physical form. There would always be a connection, but not this kind of bond.

"Ooh," Muse cried out as she tumbled over and experienced her first, but hopefully not her last orgasm. "Can we do that again?"

"Mmhm. All night long, if you want. Sleep is overrated," Abby answered.

"I've tasted so many wonderful things, Abby. Can I taste one more?"

"Oh, um, do you mean…" Abby stammered.

"Yes," Muse responded as she flipped Abby on her back and started to traverse her body. The slightly sweet taste of Abby surprised Muse. Although it wasn't the same kind of sweet as the desserts she'd had, it was definitely more on the sweet versus tangy side. Instead of the musty odor she thought she would find, Muse was delighted when Abby reminded her of the cookie she'd eaten when they had their picnic. She felt compelled to share that thought. "You smell like cookies."

Abby laughed. "If you're going to continue a verbal commentary…oh…never mind…" Abby's hips began to lift, and Muse knew at that moment that whatever she was doing with her tongue was having the same effect as when Abby had touched her earlier. Abby's gyrations increased until Muse heard a long, low moan escape, and she felt her relax against the bed. A tapping on her shoulders and a gentle tug brought Muse back, and then they were kissing again.

"I wish we had started making love the very first night. I've wasted so much time," Muse lamented.

"Like I said before, we have all night."

CHAPTER TEN

The stark reality of the day did not hit Abby until a small light from the opening in her blinds fell across her eyes. Plato enjoyed looking out the window and had pawed at the blinds until a small corner bent back, creating the large hole. They'd made love until the wee hours of the morning until both women fell asleep from exhaustion. At first, the reality of the new day did not hit Abby until her grogginess had subsided.

The pit in the bottom of her stomach grew with the realization that Muse was leaving today. Their time had run out. Abby had met the perfect woman, finally, and she wasn't a woman at all. She wasn't sure what Muse was. A concept. A fantasy. A spirit. Some kind of higher power. It didn't matter what she was because, in a few short hours, she would be no more.

Abby allowed the water in her eyes to stream down her face. Never in her life had she felt such despair. Muse shifted beside her, and her eyes blinked open. At first, they seemed unfocused. Then sadness appeared as Muse reached to brush away Abby's tears.

"Don't cry, Abby."

"You're leaving today. You can't ask me to shut down my feelings about that."

"I'm sorry. I'm not leaving you."

"You're not?" Abby's relief was palpable.

"No, I'll always be with you in the same way as I've been there with you from the very beginning. Remember that first spark of inspiration when you were six, and you wrote the short story you were so proud to show your father?"

The women continued to lie in bed, facing each other. Abby nodded her head and smiled. "The one about the princess storming the castle to save the maiden from the Tyrannosaurus Rex? I have to give kudos to my father for not blinking an eye at that storyline. He merely chuckled. He'd taken me to the dinosaur exhibit the day before, and I suppose the fierce dinosaur made an impression. Even at a young age, I had an alternate view of who should save the fair maiden. He never cared that I was a lesbian."

"Your father was a great supporter of your imagination. That always made my job a lot easier."

"You being there like before is not the same as you being here with me now. We made love all night because I'm falling for you. How can I possibly be inspired now if you leave?"

"I think your block will end quickly. Trust me on this. I've seen this happen before."

"You mean heartbreak. Don't you?" Abby asked.

Muse wouldn't meet Abby's eyes. "Yes."

"I don't care about my block. Don't go back. You've broken the rules. Maybe they won't let you return."

"Tell me more about your father," Muse redirected.

Abby knew what Muse was doing. She was a master at taking the conversation in a different direction. For now, she decided that it wasn't a bad idea. Distraction was the only thing left. A Band-Aid on a painful gash, but it was better than nothing. She was resigned to the fact that Muse would leave today.

"He wasn't perfect. Who is? But he did the best he could in a less than perfect situation. I had to be a constant reminder of what he'd lost."

"Your mother."

Abby nodded. "I saw their wedding pictures and the pictures of when she was pregnant with me. She was so beautiful, and my father was beaming at her in every photo."

"He did not try to replace your mother after she died giving birth to you?"

"No, not even when I stomped my feet and begged for him to give me a mommy for Christmas. All the other kids had a mommy, and I thought he was simply being mean because he'd never gotten one for me. Like he could go to the corner store and pick one up for half price if he waited until Christmas Eve. I told him I would smash my piggy and help him buy one if he couldn't afford a new mommy. He just looked at me with unshed tears and said that all the money in the world would never be able to replace my mother because she was priceless. I left him alone after that because he seemed so sad, and I never wanted to see him like that again."

"I never knew that."

"It happened when I was five. Before that first awful story that I wrote." Abby chuckled.

"Oh, we knew right away you would be one of my subjects. For a six-year-old, the story was quite inventive. I'm surprised you never wrote about your dad. There were some amusing stories over the years. I remember when he tried to explain menstruation with you when you turned thirteen."

"I almost forgot about that. My father caught me rinsing my panties in the sink and turned around, not saying a word. Thirty minutes later, he returned with a box of maxi pads and asked if I had a moment to talk."

Muse laughed. "The look on your face was more panicked than his."

"Yeah, I remember the only thought in my head was a hard 'no.' He scrubbed his face trying to find a way to start the conversation. I never wanted a mother more than on that day, and I think he knew that."

"It didn't stop him from giving you the textbook version of when a girl becomes a woman."

"When I found the book that he'd apparently purchased years before, I had to laugh. He must have memorized the phrases to use. That was the most painful discussion we ever had. He did, however, manage to avoid the whole conventional sex talk. I guess he figured that wasn't as important since he'd already concluded I was a lesbian and probably not at risk for pregnancy. Thanks for distracting me, but can I ask you a question? Is there any possibility you could return, um, you know as the Muse I know instead of a vague concept?"

Muse caressed Abby's face. "Honestly, I don't know. I'm not sure what will happen when I return. I only know I'm having very conflicted feelings. I don't want to be the cause of so many losing their purpose in life or at best, seriously dampening it. I've caused enough chaos."

"When will you leave?"

Muse glanced at the hole in the blinds. "I should return to the beach in another hour. Don't come with me. That would be more than I can handle. I'll leave the motorcycle."

"Okay. How about one last breakfast?"

"No, I would prefer making love again. Breakfast, I can do without. The physical closeness one last time will hopefully be enough to give me the strength I need to leave."

****

Abby knew it was a bad idea, but a compulsion to sneak away to the beach and watch Muse leave came over her. She could not deny herself one last moment. As Abby ran in the direction Muse had taken, a piece of driftwood in her path caused Abby to tumble forward. The last thing she saw before spitting sand was Muse fading from view. Abby flipped onto her back and squinted as the sun's brightness hit her eyes. Sitting, she began sobbing on the beach and didn't stop until an elderly gentleman approached.

"Are you all right, my dear?" His knees creaked as he slowly squatted in front of her. "Your head is bleeding. Let me help."

Abby touched her forehead and felt the familiar stickiness. She brought her hand to her line of vision and noted the red stain on her fingertips. Those same fingers that had brought Muse to a glorious climax only thirty minutes earlier.

"I'll be fine. My house is not far from here." She thought of how Muse had patched her before, and now she would have to reapply the glue herself. A new round of tears exploded from her eyes.

"I'll walk you home," the man offered.

"No, really, I'd rather you not."

The man pulled a clean handkerchief from his pocket and handed it to her. "At least take this. My father always taught me to carry one in case I could be of assistance to a damsel in distress." He smiled. "I believe you fit the bill."

Abby accepted his offering. "Thank you. You remind me of my father."

"And you remind me of my daughter."

"He died a few years ago," Abby blurted.

"So did my daughter. Cancer."

"Same."

"Are you sure I can't walk you home?" he asked.

"All right. Maybe this is a sign. I was just talking about my father to someone very special to me. I've never seen you on this beach before. Are you new?"

The man shrugged. "In a manner of speaking. I'm on a short vacation. I've been searching for something. Answers maybe, and then I saw you fall. This does seem like serendipity." The man offered his hand, and Abby took it. She needed something stable right now, and since she wasn't ready to spill her guts to her best friend, this stranger would have to do.

"I'm Abby. I appreciate your kindness."

"Nice to meet you, Abby. Peter." He offered his body for Abby to lean on, which was surprisingly sturdy. The pair walked carefully on the path to Abby's house.

***

"Ah, so you've returned." Zeus sighed. "Sorry, I was unable to greet you. I had another issue to resolve. You're on probation," he declared with a fair amount of irritation to his voice. "Not only did you violate several rules, but you stepped completely out of your wheelhouse when you sent that man, Peter, to Abby. Our inspiration is limited to artistic endeavors."

"She misses her father. I thought it would help." Muse shimmered uncomfortably in front of her boss.

"You need to work again with Inspiration Mexico. I want you back on track as soon as possible."

"Calli? I don't think she is too happy with me right now. Why do you insist on calling her Inspiration Mexico? Her name is Calli."

"She is not as unhappy with you as I am. How is it that you have influenced her, but she has not swayed you? I'm disappointed in both of you." Zeus narrowed his eyes.

"Can you please call us by our names and not Inspiration Mexico and Inspiration Northwest? Referring to us by our region is so impersonal for such a personal job."

"Very well. I'll use your names if it's that important to you. I don't know why you let your subjects tempt you so greatly."

"I think I'll be much better at my job with my experience. Even though all I seem to be inspiring are works of art that are the very definition of despair and sadness. I do, however, see a few masterpieces in the future of those works. Even in the beginning stages, the trajectory is clear."

"Was it worth almost losing your position?"

Muse smiled. "It was—every single moment. I almost wish you'd decided not to let me return. A huge part of me was willing to sacrifice all my subjects, but then I thought of how that would have impacted Abby, and I couldn't do that to her. I couldn't take away her purpose. That would have been selfish of me and profoundly unfair."

He nodded. "And that's the only reason I've allowed you to return. You've always had such a large impact on your subjects. That would be hard to replace, and your absence would cause too much strain on the others. And the result would be too many dancing along the edges causing them to lose their gift. We've already been dealing with that as this new e-book craze floods the market. This has caused an alarming crisis of faith. The writers are dropping like flies. Some of the best are no longer working their craft."

"I know. Do you think it would be possible for me to ever—"

"No, you cannot take another vacation. I should never have approved this one. The havoc you created will remain for a very long time. We simply don't have the resources to meet the needs that arise during your absence." He shook his head.

CHAPTER ELEVEN

Three days had passed since Muse left. Three days. The thought that this was the same short time frame she'd had with Muse caused a brand-new round of tears. Abby sat in her bed with her laptop propped on her thighs. Through her bleary eyes, she was typing furiously. All of her emotions transferred to the screen in front of her. The words were sad and depressing, but they were definitely her best work.

Abby shouldn't have been surprised to hear the loud banging on her front door. Not wanting to answer her phone after Jenny left nearly a hundred combinations of voice and text messages, Abby had turned off her phone and let the battery deplete. She groaned as she tossed the covers aside and shuffled to answer the door. She knew if she tried to ignore the loud banging, Jenny would search for her spare key and bust inside. Abby wanted to present a semblance of normalcy. It didn't matter that this was only the second time in her life she'd gone three days without a shower. At first, she'd been able to detect the rank smell, but over the last twenty-four hours, the stink had dissipated as she got used to her sour odor.

After Abby opened the door, Jenny barged in. She tilted her head and declared, "Holy shit. You look like death." She sniffed the air. "What is that foul smell? Did you forget to put away some meat? It's making me nauseous."

"It's probably me. I haven't showered in a few days."

"You what?"

"I've been writing. A writer has to take advantage of when inspiration chooses to visit." And with that, Abby burst into tears.

Jenny quickly pulled Abby into a hug and began rubbing her back. "I'm going to kick Muse's very fine ass. I knew something was off when you two came to dinner. That little slut. Where did she scurry off to? I don't care how far away she lives. I'm going to track her lying, cheating ass down."

"Lying, cheating ass?" Abby pushed away. "She didn't lie to me or cheat. And you can't track her down because I don't know where she's gone."

"What's her last name? Muse is such an unusual name. All we have to do is use one of the websites on Google. I'll have her location in a matter of minutes."

"Doubtful."

"Gave you a false name, huh? She *did* lie to you. I'm gonna rip her tits off."

"She didn't exactly give me a fake name. It's complicated. She doesn't have a last name."

"That's ridiculous. Everyone has a last name."

"Madonna, Cher, the symbol that was formerly Prince?"

"Are you telling me Muse is a celebrity?"

"In a manner of speaking, I suppose so. Muse's job is vital, and she had to return."

"So what, you're a writer. You can live anywhere. I can't believe I'm saying this because I'll miss you like mad. But Abby, I promise we won't lose touch like before. I won't let that happen again. You're too important to me."

"This can't be fixed by geography," Abby insisted.

"As angry as I am at her right now, there is one thing I know for sure. In all the years I've known you, I've never, ever, seen you look at someone like you did with Muse. I may not be wise about many things, but I know love when I see it."

Abby turned and limped slowly to her couch, slumping into the cushions, hoping somehow, they would swallow her whole and take her to wherever Muse's essence manifested.

"I know, and the really horrible thing is I never told her. Now I won't get the chance. I think she left because she was afraid of what might happen, not just with me but others who depended on her. You know, I would have given up my writing for her. It's a sacrifice I was willing to make, and I didn't let her know that."

"Oh, hon." Jenny sat next to Abby and patted her back. "True love always wins out. We'll find a way to track her down so you can tell her everything you just admitted to me."

Abby let a weak smile appear on her face. "I think she knows, Jenny. Somehow, I think she knows."

"How is that possible?"

"We sort of travel in the same circles. I'm sure it's evident in my writing."

"Wow, that's fast. I didn't know it was possible to write a whole book in three days. Unless it's a short story. You don't write a lot of those. Did you do one for a major compilation? Maybe whoever you sent the draft to knows how to get in touch."

"No, that won't happen. You're going to have to trust me on this," Abby declared with certainty.

"First things first. You need a shower before any scheming. My nostrils are burning. You stink. And, girlfriend, I could fry an egg with the grease in your hair. It's not an attractive look. You cannot pull off dreads. Just saying, that's for the young people, and even on them, I don't like the look."

Abby laughed for the first time in three days. She didn't know if she was ready to move on, but it was a start.

***

Calli appeared in front of Muse. A look of pity etched across her face. "Zeus sent me to ascertain how you're doing and make sure you're back on track. I'm supposed to do whatever it takes. How do you think your first week is going? Anything I can help with? I thought maybe we could develop a performance improvement plan together."

"Why? My subjects are writing, painting, sculpting, creating, so I don't need a plan," Muse insisted.

"I know you don't believe that. You aren't blind. You've been following Abby, and she's the worst of them all. I'm ready to slit my wrists after reading her stuff. That's how depressing her new short story was." Calli held out her arms for further emphasis.

"She'll conquer this. She has before. After her father died, she went through a phase, but she made it to the other side. I think writing helps her work through her issues. She'll be back to her signature genre after a bit. Sometimes it's good to explore something new. She's very good at dramatic fiction. I shouldn't discourage that, even if I knew how."

"You keep telling yourself that, but it doesn't make it true. Your bleak mood is not only affecting Abby, but it's spilling into your subjects. They are starting to notice. Do you know what the news people are saying now?"

Muse shook her head.

"They've been parading artist after artist before the camera to repeat their stories of woe. Dark, depressing paintings. Grotesque sculptures and romance stories without happy endings. One writer who is a notorious plodder had her story mapped out until seven days ago when she made an abrupt turnaround and changed the ending. She killed off the main characters and explained to her publisher the ending was life. People die. End of story. They can't publish that drivel. The readers will form a mutiny and boycott her books." Calli's voice had risen until by the end she was screeching.

"What's so wrong with a bit of reality now and again? Stories can't always have happy endings." Muse crossed her arms. Ever since her three-day vacation, she had adopted so many of the mannerisms of her subjects. For some reason, Calli crossed her arms. Muse wondered if it was a way for Calli to show empathy. That was new. She always felt Calli's support, and sometimes it almost felt like love, but lately, her gestures were amplified and obvious. Muse wondered if she had started a new trend with all the Inspirations or just the ones who tended to have territories with the more dramatic artists.

Calli sighed. "How about you concentrate on happy thoughts? Why don't you try to channel your night of passion with Abby? Maybe if you remember that, you'll do a better job of inspiring your subjects."

"How about you allow me to revisit Abby and divide my work amongst the others for a short time? You know that sometimes the humans cover for one another on vacation? It seems to help when they return, limiting the stacks of papers and emails that a person has to come back to. I think we should think about that system for us." Abby looked hopefully at Calli.

Calli scoffed, "Our subjects don't cover for each other. No one picks up the slack when a writer has a block, or a painter stops midway through their painting."

"Haven't you heard of co-authors? Or how about musicians who collaborate? You know that framing a painting is as important to the piece's overall effect as the painting alone. Art is never created in a vacuum."

Calli tapped her chin. "Hmmm. Okay, you've made some very valid points. But what if everyone wants to take these little mini-vacations to recharge their batteries or whatever it is you did down there? That's not going to solve the fundamental problem. You fell in love with one of your subjects. Admit it. Another excursion will only make matters worse for you and her."

Muse didn't care anymore. She let the tears fall freely. "I know. I don't know what to do, just leave me alone."

Calli shuffled her feet. "I'm not going to make any promises, but let me see what can be done?"

Muse looked up, and hope, along with tears, filled her eyes.

***

Erato wrung her hands in distress as she approached her favorite sister. "Calli, you must do something about Musetta. The darkness is causing a ripple of concern. If it were only Melpomene raising a ruckus, I would not be so worried, after all tragedy is her area. But Euterpe feels the same, and her poetry is supposed to bring delight. I admit I share their unease."

"I've been monitoring her work and am aware of the situation. Even the comedy clubs are affected by Muse's mood. Her heart is broken. She asked for another vacation. I told her I would help, but what can I possibly do? A vacation will only make matters worse. The only solution is to reunite her with Abigail Prentice, resulting in a whole other passel of problems. What do you suggest?"

"Talk with Zeus. He allowed me to marry Malos," Erato suggested.

"That's different. We benefited from diversity in our lineage, and as an ancient, you can walk in both worlds without consequence."

"If we lose Musetta as we lost Dumi, so be it. Perhaps there is another solution. Advocate for another three days to allow Musetta a chance to resolve this crisis. She is creative. Perhaps she will think of something we have not considered."

Calli nodded. "Very well. I will ask Zeus for an audience. Perhaps if I mention I have the support of all of my sisters, he will be persuaded to grant her this extra time."

"I will make sure that all of us concur." Erato hugged Calli before walking toward her other sisters, who had materialized inside a blue mist.

***

The only reason Jenny agreed to leave was because Abby had promised to recharge her phone and take a shower. Not much had changed since Jenny left, except now Abby knew if she wanted to avoid another confrontation with Jenny, she had to respond to her best friend's text messages. They were mostly asking how she was to which she simply replied *okay*.

She tried to rationalize that all she was doing was stretching the truth a bit. In reality, Abby was far from okay.

Seven more days had passed, and Abby had taken one shower when it was clear that Plato wouldn't snuggle with her until she cleaned herself up. Wearing the same pair of sweats, she shuffled robotically from the bedroom to the bathroom. Occasionally Abby made her way to the kitchen for coffee and enough food to keep her from passing out. For the first time in her life, she wished she lived in a large city where she could remain in her house and never leave. City dwellers could order groceries or take out for delivery. She didn't have that option. Not to mention, the town busybodies would notice she hadn't been to the store in over ten days. That news would get back to Jenny.

She wasn't surprised to hear the telltale banging on her door a week later. After opening the door, she turned and walked away, refusing to meet Jenny's eyes. She headed for the refrigerator and the open bottle of wine. It wasn't noon yet, but she didn't care. She'd broken the no-alcohol-before-noon rule several days ago, and she knew today was going to be a day for liquid numbing.

"No lectures, please."

"Well, it's a little early for me, but sure, I'll take a glass," Jenny deadpanned.

"No, you certainly will not. I'm not about to drag you into my pit of gloom."

"Well, I'm not letting you go there alone." Jenny had four Thriftway bags dangling from her arms.

"Fine, you win." Abby smacked the bottle of wine on the counter, causing a loud clang. Plato ran from the room and presumably hid in the bedroom.

Jenny made her victory face. "Did you honestly think I was going to buy your bullshit texts? Gloria said you haven't been to the store in ten days. She wondered if you were ill."

"Gloria should mind her own damn business."

Jenny began putting away the groceries. "You're welcome. I purchased food you don't have to prepare. Easy stuff that you can grab and eat. I thought I would start slow with items like hummus, feta, olives, and tomatoes, and cheese for grilled cheese sandwiches with tomato soup. I know that there is a tiny bit of effort to make the grilled cheese and soup, but I thought you could work up to it."

"You shouldn't have." Abby shuffled to the couch and sat.

Jenny paused, turned her head in Abby's direction and glared. "Are you freakin' kidding me? There is nothing, and I mean nothing, in your refrigerator but condiments. What are you doing? Eating mayonnaise and ketchup? You don't even have any bread or butter. Starving yourself to death is not the answer. You better at least be feeding Plato, or I'm calling the Humane Society and reporting you for animal cruelty."

"Plato is fine. I can't believe you would think I was neglecting him."

"You know who else you're letting down?"

"I thought I said no lectures."

"I never agreed to that. Nat. That's who. She's going to leave for college soon, and she misses you."

"You don't fight fair." Abby wagged her finger at Jenny.

"No, I admit I don't. Maybe you should make an appointment to see someone. You're starting to scare me, Abby. Really scare me. Remember when David was talking about this weird thing that happened with art and how he thought it was a kind of mass hysteria?"

Abby perked up for a second and was too curious not to ask Jenny to continue. "Yeah, is it still happening?"

"Not exactly the same thing where no one is writing or painting or whatever. It's kind of worse. Everything is coming out dark and dreary. It's like every single artist in the Pacific Northwest has had their heart ripped out. It's weird." Jenny pulled her tablet from her shoulder bag and touched her CNN app. "Come, take a look at this."

Abby shuffled to Jenny's side where she could see the video.

Show Host: *My guests are a scientist, a liberal pundit, and a conservative expert. What is your assessment of what has been happening over the last ten days in the Northwest? It's all over social media. Every new painting lacks color. The shades of black and gray are not artistic, like in black and white photos, they are merely depressing. All the poems, short stories, and teasers on books feature despair, loneliness, and depression. I've never seen anything quite like this in all my years.*

Political Correspondent: *Art imitates life. Clearly, the rhetoric of the President has had a profound impact on the arts.*

Show Host: *Dr. Carlson, you've theorized there is a kind of hysteria infecting the masses as it relates to this disturbing trend with the arts. You've blamed the media for their excessive reporting on this latest phenomenon.*

Dr. Carlson: *Yes, it's quite simple. If I tell you to look around the room and find everything that's the color blue, you're easily able to do that. Now, if I ask you to close your eyes. Please, humor me and close your eyes.*

Show Host chuckles nervously and closes his eyes.

Dr. Carlson: *Now, please tell me all those items in this studio that are the color red.*

Show Host pauses: *Uh, my tie has red in it, I think.*

Dr. Carlson: *Do you see how difficult that was? It's because I first asked you to focus on the color blue. This is the real danger of media. It can profoundly affect the perspective of the masses. A theory is planted in a group's head, and the result is groupthink.*

Show Host: *Interesting. I suppose that makes it very important for the media to stick with the facts. However, we're in an era of not only reporting facts, but as we are doing now, examining them more closely. As long as all perspectives are presented, this evolution is healthy for the people. I don't believe the media has only put forward dark and dreary facts and analysis. However, this odd phenomenon that is happening is factual and, frankly, a bit scary. I don't believe I'm in the minority when I state I'd rather not fill my bookshelves or cover my walls with any art coming out lately. Right now, it feels more like mass hysteria than groupthink.*

Republican Pundit: *The only mass hysteria happening right now is the political tribalism of the left. I've watched how the liberal media attaches every single negative movement in our country to the President, and that's ludicrous.*

Political Correspondent: *How can you possibly ignore his hateful tweets and incendiary words at his rallies. Make no mistake, the despair and darkness are a direct result of how he leads this country into a black hole. His slogan should have been* Make America Hate Again.

Republican Pundit: *Now who is spewing hate and discontent? The left continued to call our fine President a traitor, even though the special prosecutor's report indicated no collusion, no obstruction.*

Dr. Carlson: *I believe we should be cautious about our reporting. An interesting case of mass hysteria occurred in the Northwest back in the 50s, proving the Northwest is quite susceptible to this phenomenon. It was dubbed the "Seattle Windshield Pitting Epidemic." Starting in Bellingham, people began to notice pits and dings in their windshields. This observation spread to other communities in Washington and led to theories as wild as cosmic rays, sand fleas, or the new million-watt radio transfer. Before all was said and done, over 3,000 windshields were reported damaged, and both the Governor, Arthur B. Langlie, and President Dwight D. Eisenhower were contacted for assistance. The Seattle police eventually determined it was 5% vandalism and 95% hysteria.*

Show Host: *Interesting. Thank you, as always, for your contributions.*

Jenny shifted in her seat and then put away her tablet. "Abby, I think I might be one of those people who have been affected by mass hysteria because I'm starting to theorize that Muse had something to do with what is happening. The timing is perfect. She arrived at the same time all this crazy shit started happening, then when she left, and you went dark, so did the art. Tell me I'm nuts. Tell me it's all a weird coincidence."

***

Perhaps it was the opening Jenny had given Abby. Or it could have been her desperate need to talk to someone other than a kind stranger—a person she trusted instantly like when she'd met Muse. By the time Jenny turned her focus on Abby and looked into her eyes, Abby decided she would confess, regardless of how crazy it would sound. She needed someone else to know the secret and to help her work through it. Obviously, she was doing a shitty job of surfacing on the other side of the tunnel.

Abby pushed her greasy hair away from her face and stated with conviction, "It's not a weird coincidence."

Jenny's mouth hung open. "It's not?"

Abby shook her head. "This is going to sound bonkers, and trust me when I say I understand how difficult it is to believe me, but Muse is Inspiration."

"I don't understand." The worry lines in Jenny's forehead deepened.

"I'll tell you what Muse told me. Remember those old movies about Death taking a holiday? This time, Inspiration took a vacation. Apparently, there's some truth to Greek mythology. Zeus exists."

Jenny's eyes bulged. "No way."

"Inspiration was burned out, and she decided to take a three-day holiday like Death. I'm one of her subjects. She thought that because I had such a block, she wasn't doing her job properly."

"Um, I, uh, I don't know what to say to that," Jenny sputtered.

"I know, right? Then I had to screw it up and fall for her. If only she had spent a few nice days here and then went back, I'd be unblocked and producing again. Instead, a shit-ton of artists are flinging mass depression, not unlike chimps tossing feces."

Jenny jumped from the couch and began pacing. "Okay, say I believe you. How come it's only happening in our neck of the woods?"

"I guess there is more than one Inspiration. They have territories."

Jenny stopped pacing. "You're shitting me?"

"Nope."

Jenny grinned. "So, are they all women, or are there some hot men in other territories? Should I move and become an artist?"

"I thought you were gaga over David?"

"Oh, I am, but a woman has to keep her options open."

As depressed as Abby felt about losing Muse, Jenny always managed to make her laugh. "Do you know how much I adore you?"

"I do. Okay, we need to make a plan to get Muse back. I don't want her to grab you like Death did, so we need a different ending here."

Abby shook her head sadly. "I don't think she can return. I probably shouldn't have told you. She broke their rules by telling me and then, uh…"

Jenny slapped her hand against her mouth. "You slept with her, didn't you?" She walked over and patted Abby's shoulder. "Oh my, I am so proud of you. You're like my perfect prodigy. You got Inspiration to have sex with you."

"We made love," Abby corrected.

Jenny waved her hand in the air. "Yeah, yeah, same thing."

"Not the same thing. But the point is, Muse was at risk of being, well, fired for lack of terminology. She said something about them not allowing her to return, but for some reason, that didn't happen. Even though she broke their rules."

"Good, good, that's probably key. Maybe if Muse returns, she'll be able to do something so egregious, they'll force her to stay because they won't welcome her back."

"I don't know, Jenny. She was really distraught about the consequences of her not returning. She felt like it would have a profound impact. David did not help, you know, with all that talk about the end of civilization."

Jenny sat next to Abby and patted her knee. "Oh, I love David, but he can be *soooo* dramatic. Inspiration is in territories, right?"

"Uh-huh."

"Why can't they reassign the Northwest? You know, divvy it up?"

Abby scratched her itchy head. She really needed to take another shower. "The job has expanded over the years with more artists, and I don't think the other Inspirations can handle any more work. It sounds like they're overwhelmed now, and if Muse left, they'd be short-staffed."

"Well, welcome to my world. 'Do more with less' is the mantra. I hear that every frickin' day. Surely, if health care has been able to figure it out, Inspiration should find a way. They need an efficiency expert. You know, a way to enable them to be more productive."

"Don't you think if there was a way to make them more efficient, they would have already thought of that solution? The fact that they took Muse back after she broke the rules is probably the best indication that was not an option."

"I suppose you're right. Maybe that's why the administrators keep the dead weight at our hospital. But you know what? I don't think a warm body is better than no body. I'd rather work extra hours than have an incompetent tech doing images."

"Muse is not incompetent."

"No, but I don't think she wants to continue doing what she's been doing anymore, and that's just as bad. A disengaged worker is as destructive as an inept one. You go take a shower, stinky, while I prepare food for us and think about this a bit."

Abby grabbed Jenny, and fiercely embraced her. "I love you. Sorry for being such a Debbie Downer and for my appalling hygiene. I hope my stinkiness didn't get on you."

Jenny grinned after Abby let go. "It probably did, but you're forgiven. I don't trust you to take care of yourself, so I'm helping myself to your extra house key. Don't even think about denying me that tiny bit of insurance."

"Okay." Abby's watery eyes met Jenny's. "It's in the top drawer next to the stove. I'd rather you take that one instead of the one hidden in the rock outside."

"Sneaky. I figured you had one given your talent of locking yourself out. However, I am aware of the extra one in your drawer. I've been to your house many times before. I know where you keep everything." She grinned.

CHAPTER TWELVE

Jenny and Abby walked arm in arm down the beach. After her shower and a comfort meal of grilled cheese sandwiches and tomato soup, Jenny had convinced Abby to soak up some vitamin D and come on a short walk with her. Abby had to admit, it felt good to be in the sunshine again. Walking on the beach had always been a way to clear her head and rejuvenate her whenever she was stuck. Most of the time, it worked like a charm, however the strategy had not worked during her long stretch of writer's block before Muse appeared.

"So, I was thinking. What if there were a way to expand the reach of Inspiration through social media? Why can't the Inspirations develop soldiers or minions to do their bidding? Surely, they aren't the only ones to influence artists. You belong to writers' groups, don't you?"

"Yeah. There was this author who started Writing Wednesdays. We had to report to each other how many words were written. We'd go on writing sprints. It helped when I was only partially blocked. It did not help when there was a full press clogging."

"Okay, okay." Jenny nodded. "See, I think this whole mass hysteria thing could work to our advantage. What if

Inspirations implanted these seeds in a horde of people and then caused those individuals to inspire others? You know the best leaders are not the ones who do all the work themselves but delegate that work. Leaders inspire their worker bees to accomplish everything they can't achieve entirely on their own."

"Really? Do you think that could work? I mean, I don't have much knowledge of the inner workings of the Inspirations. I only know they have territories." Abby picked up the pace and turned her head to the vast beach in front of her.

At first, Abby thought she was dreaming when Muse appeared from the mist, and then she heard two words that were absolute magic to her ears.

"Hello, Abby," Muse said.

Abby let go of Jenny's arm and started running toward Muse, but before she could reach her, she slipped on a piece of seaweed and fell on her ass. She was not about to be deterred by her fall as she quickly jumped up, brushed off the sand, and leaped into Muse's arms before she had a chance to express concern.

"Good thing I took a shower earlier."

Muse stroked the side of Abby's face when Abby let go of her death grip on Muse. "You are lovely now, and you were still beautiful, even without a shower. You didn't injure yourself again, did you?"

"Only my pride."

Jenny approached and laughed. "Classic Abby. I have to tell you she wasn't very lovely an hour ago, but now I know you truly care for Abby. Even without the dark art coming out of the Northwest, I'd know that look of love anywhere.

Damn, I could almost feel that caress to Abby's face from several feet away."

"Hello, Jenny. You have fascinating ideas."

"Were you spying on us?" Jenny narrowed her eyes.

Muse's laughter floated in the breeze. "Spying is such an ugly word. We keep tabs."

"Then you'll know the horrible things happening in the Northwest. If I can't pick up a romance from my favorite Northwest author and get my happily ever after, there's going to be a bloodbath of epic proportions. Readers will begin rioting in the streets."

"I know, I know. I haven't been myself lately. Can we finish the walk? I've missed this beach."

"You're gonna fix this, aren't you?" Jenny placed her hands on her hips and glared at Muse.

"For now, I have three more days to figure things out. My colleagues are not happy with me. Bunch of whiny babies. They were grumbling so loud, that I'm amazed you didn't hear them."

"Is that what happened this morning?" Jenny asked.

"What?" Abby turned to her friend.

"Oh, while you were taking your shower, you should have seen the storm. It was the freakiest thing. The sun was shining, and then suddenly, the clouds rolled in, and bam" — Jenny smacked her hand— "thunder and lightning. I didn't think a whole lot about it because you know Forks, the weather changes on a dime, even in the summer."

"The weather goddesses are going to be pissed. They don't like it when others mess with what they consider solely within their domain."

"There are weather goddesses?" Jenny and Abby asked in unison.

Muse laughed. "Gotcha!"

"Ha ha, a real comedian. Well, you certainly haven't helped those writers lately. I heard the comedy clubs were some of the hardest hit." Jenny glared.

"Really, you heard that?" Abby asked.

Jenny put out her hands. "Kidding. See, two can play that game."

"Actually, you were right. That was the final straw. Calli gets a real kick from the comedians. She was most disturbed by what was happening to them during my dark period."

"Um, hey, I forgot I had this, uh, thing, with Nat and David today. I gotta shove off. You going to be okay?" Jenny asked.

The first genuine smile in nearly two weeks appeared on Abby's face. "Yes. I'll call you later."

***

The day seemed a tiny amount brighter than the last time Muse had visited. She took Abby's hand and reveled in the sensation of reconnecting with her. Desperately wanting to confess her love had almost caused Muse to blurt those three little words. Inspiration was in a precarious position right now. The experiment—that's what they were calling it. Her boss intended to see how everything would evolve. Nothing had changed for Inspiration in over a millennium. Could they learn something from their subjects? Could this be more of a partnership? Her boss was skeptical. Calli had sided with Muse, and she was grateful for what Calli had achieved. Regardless of what ultimately happened, she would forever be grateful for this additional time. And, maybe they could find a way to make it work.

"How have you been?" Abby asked.

"Not so good. Wasn't that evident?"

"I'm so sorry." Abby stopped and pierced Muse with such a pained expression that it broke Muse's heart.

"Definitely not your fault, and I saw what I did to you. Abby, I don't know how in the world I can fix this. I'm the one who should be apologizing."

"How much did you see? I suppose I knew you were keeping tabs on me, but I thought because you have so many other subjects, you'd be too distracted to see how far I'd fallen. At least you weren't able to smell me from wherever you went."

"It's hard to explain. We're acutely aware of all of our subjects, but sometimes we're hyper-aware of a few over others. We're not supposed to have our favorites, but we all do. You've always been one of mine." Muse smiled to remove any real criticism. "I think taking a shower every day is important."

"What now?"

"I won't try to deceive you and tell you these next three days aren't very important. They are monitoring my subjects, including you. I've requested that you not be assigned to another. Calli offered, but I declined. I'm conducting my own research. I don't want to influence you, unduly, with exactly what that experiment entails. Suffice it to say, the next three days won't simply be fun and games."

"What do you mean?"

"You can't entertain me twenty-four/seven. I want you to continue to write. Perhaps you can toss that drivel you wrote after I left?"

Abby dramatically clutched her chest and then smiled. "Everyone's a critic."

"I tried to rationalize that it was perfect, award-winning material. It made me cry harder. I didn't want that for your readers. That isn't what you write. We have enough non-fiction writers and others who write a bit too much reality for my taste."

"No matter what happens, I won't write that same depressing shit I wrote before. I'd rather give up writing than cause you any more distress than I have already."

"What would your day normally be like if you were inspired to write? How many hours do you spend on your craft?"

"There is no normal for me. If I'm on a roll, I can spend nearly all day writing with short breaks in-between. Other days, I'll write in the morning, then take a long break and return to writing for a few hours in the evening. I would say this pattern is more typical than writing the whole day. I'm not going to squander my limited time with you, though. Please don't ask me to do that. How about if I write a couple hours a day for the next three days and spend the rest of the time with you? Will that work?"

"Yeah, that will work." Muse spun Abby around and pulled her close for a surprise kiss. She'd wanted to do that the minute she laid eyes on her but thought it better to test the waters first. She knew how hurt Abby was and thought she might be blamed for the pain.

"Wow! What was that for, not that I'm complaining or anything?" Abby caressed the side of Muse's face and pressed her lips to Muse's briefly enough to solidify her response.

"I missed you so much, and I really missed kissing you."

"Is that all you missed doing with me?" Abby grinned.

Muse blushed. "No, but I don't want you to think we'll spend the entire three days making love. I need us to talk more, and I plan to ask you about social media."

"Okay, as long as you reciprocate. There are so many questions that I have and didn't get the chance to ask. We had so little time left, and I had such a craving to connect with you."

"I understand. Talking is intimate, but touching can take things to a new level, right?" Abby took Muse's hand and began to walk with her.

"For me, yes. I've always felt very vulnerable when making love. Not having clothes on doesn't just mean you're exposed to the elements, but you're more exposed to the scrutiny of others. I feel the same way every time a new book of mine is published. Everyone is getting a peek into my innermost thoughts and feelings. When a writer produces fiction, a major part of themselves is woven into each character. Even those characters who are the villains provide an insight into the author. When I write about what I abhor the most, I concentrate those characteristics on the villains. As for my flawed main characters, those flaws are frequently my flaws. The less flawed characters often possess the characteristics I strive to have."

"I've noticed. Do you sometimes work through issues that cause you distress?"

Abby chuckled. "Sometimes. Never piss off a writer. They'll make you the villain in their next story."

"Was I going to be a villain?" Muse saw the large piece of driftwood they'd first sat against when Abby had shared the first sunset. She turned slightly to lead Abby to the same spot.

"No, never."

"But I hurt you."

Abby shook her head. "No, your leaving hurt. *You* didn't hurt me. There is a huge difference."

"I could have refused to go back. I didn't choose you. How is that not an unforgivable choice?"

"Because you were thinking of the greater good. How could I fault you for such an altruistic decision? I assume you're heading in the direction of that piece of driftwood for a reason."

Muse smiled. "Yes, I would like to sit in the same spot as where we spent our first night. Is that corny?"

"No, that's perfect. We should go to bed early, and instead of watching the sunset tonight, we can see the sunrise. You never got to do that."

"I would like that very much."

***

Muse grinned at Abby after taking another bite of the quick dinner Abby had prepared for the two of them. They had spent the entire afternoon on the beach. Abby cringed and looked at Muse to make sure she wasn't close to stomping from the house and never returning.

"Really, this is fine. Stop apologizing already," Muse insisted.

"In my defense, I never thought you would return, and I did offer to take you to dinner." Abby speared a cherry tomato and popped it in her mouth.

Muse laughed. "This is good. I've never had a modified Greek salad."

"You've never had a lot of different foods. Stop being so polite. At least without the onions, we can kiss and not repel one another. And, bonus, neither of us will smell like onions." Abby slammed her hand against her mouth. "I can't believe I just said that. I mean, we don't have to, you know…"

Muse smiled. "Why not? So, is this what you eat when you're on a roll with writing, feta, olives, and tomatoes in a balsamic dressing?"

"Uh-huh," Abby mumbled around a bite of the salad.

"I get not having onions, but why not cucumbers? They're not offensive."

"I don't know." Abby lifted her shoulders. "I suppose I've never thought cucumbers had much flavor. Why go to all the work of cutting them if they aren't going to add anything to the salad? I'm all about efficiency when I'm on a roll. Speaking of efficiency, I want to know everything about your job. How does creating inspiration work?"

Muse held up a finger as she finished chewing. "Have you ever wondered why an idea pops into your head, or you have a certain dream?"

"I haven't exactly devoted a ton of energy to the whys, but I suppose there are times I think about the origin of those ideas. I've certainly received questions from readers about that."

"The best way to explain things is that we are those tiny nudges. A photographer is sitting at a table, drinking her coffee, and suddenly, she feels compelled to look up at the right moment to capture the perfect photo. Bringing her camera in focus, she takes a flawless picture. The nudge happens when something inspires her to look up."

"How many subjects do you have?"

"Oh, thousands."

"Then how can you possibly nudge everyone?"

"We're very good at multitasking. It takes practice, but as you know, those tiny bits of inspiration don't happen every day. They might not happen for weeks. We are only the initial nudge. The rest flows from that spark."

"Are you saying you give us the initial idea, and then you're done?"

"No, we inspire artists to see, hear, read, or feel something at the right moment for them to envision the idea on their own. How many times have you followed a social media string that led you to your next story?"

"More than a few times. I love hanging in those groups."

"Do you know when the nudge occurs?"

"No."

"Timing is everything. I know when those discussions will take a turn, and then I nudge a person to jump onto the internet before they start scrolling through the groups. The idea is all yours. I simply help the artist open their eyes to the possibilities, to the options in front of them."

"Interesting. So, you use more than one avenue."

Muse shrugged. "Sure, the possibilities are endless. Nudge a person to go to a certain restaurant to meet a waitress they decide to paint. Inspire another to eat chili before bed, so they wake abruptly and remember that dream. Answer a phone call from your best friend to get out of the house and walk on the beach."

"You timed your return?"

Muse smiled. "I did. Inspirations work in different ways, not simply the creation of art. Although I did not inspire you to take a tumble before hugging me."

"Funny. Can I ask you another question?"

"Absolutely."

"What's it like where you, uh, hang out? I sort of have this vision of puffy white clouds and ethereal creatures floating around. I suppose not unlike some artists' visions of angels. When I met you, the first thought I had was that you were either a goddess or an angel. Then I imagined Helen of Troy, the woman who launched a thousand ships because of her beauty."

"Ah, so that's why you inquired if my name was Helen. I always wondered why you asked me that."

"What is it like?"

"I don't know how to describe it in terms you might understand. I look exactly the same here and there. Maybe we're a bit more opaque when not on earth. We don't interact with one another that much. It's a lonely existence. I think my mother mated with a human, and I hear rumors that her mother did as well. It makes sense we can so easily pass."

"You have a mother?" Abby jerked her head and looked at Muse.

"Yes, of course I had a mother. Where else do you think I came from? Just because I didn't grow up with her doesn't mean she didn't exist. Even the ancients, Calli and her eight sisters, had a mother. Although no one seems to want to talk about them. The nine ancients are a very odd bunch. I haven't interacted much with all of the ancients. If the rumors are true, they fight a lot. I suppose that's typical of sisters. The ancients are the foundation and origination of Inspiration."

"Did Death have a mother?" The question seemed to squeak out.

"Death!" Muse laughed uncontrollably. "No, he's just uh, well kind of there. Who would birth Death?"

"But you told me that your vacation was like when Death took a holiday. I don't understand." Half of Abby's face contorted in confusion.

"Hmmm. Good point. I suppose I was trying to use an example of something you might understand. In the case of Death, he had to take human form. For us, that isn't necessary. And, clearly, if the rumors are correct, we've had sex and created many offspring that are hybrids. Although, I think our awareness of ourselves and our purpose is quite a bit different. It was like one day I was called to action. I never questioned anything when I started working with Calli. I think there are many like me."

"Then why can't they simply call another to action?"

"I don't know. That's an excellent question. I should ask Calli about that."

"Before you took your jaunt on the wild side, where did you hang out, and what's it like for you in whatever place you exist?"

"We're sort of like humans mixed inside a mist or a fog."

"You move around like a mist?"

"Kind of. Like I said, it's hard to put in words that you might understand."

"And Calli is an ancient, whatever that is? She has eight sisters? Sounds like a Catholic family," Abby joked.

"Oh, they are nothing like the kind of family you're familiar with, except for their notorious bickering. Honestly, I didn't spend much time with them, only Calli. I've always simply accepted their place in history as the original source of Inspiration."

Abby's face contorted as if she were trying to figure out a complicated math problem. "You've alluded to knowing my work and many other authors. How does that work?"

"Most artists are easy to keep tabs on because once they finish their art, it's a quick glance. Writers pose unique challenges. Although, writers are amongst my favorite subjects. Since the writing process takes so long and the editing can traverse across many days, we can get into a person's head and sort of listen to the words as you reread them. Or, for industrious authors like yourself, who use programs to read back your work while editing, the almost final product is relatively clear."

"Yeah, I love my app that reads back a manuscript. I catch far more errors with that app than simply reading my final proof."

"You're one of my easier subjects because I have so many opportunities to listen."

"You mean my OCD of going through the full proof a minimum of five times?"

"Exactly."

An unfocused look appeared on Abby's face as she stared off toward the front window.

"You have an idea, don't you?"

"What? Oh, uh, sorry." Abby refocused on Muse. "Did you just do that?"

Muse half-smiled. "Sort of. It wasn't quite as defined as usual, but I did redirect your thoughts a bit, and helped you to focus on something brewing below the surface." Muse's head jerked. "Hey, I just had a surprising epiphany. If I was able to nudge you here, why couldn't I do that with others? I have an idea. Do you have an extra laptop where I can learn the ins and outs of social media?"

"Yeah."

"I want you to start writing and not lose that idea that sparked a few minutes ago, and I'll work on my own mini-inspiration."

"You wouldn't mind?"

"Of course not."

"I'm going to write our story. Maybe the ending I decide to write will come true." Abby winked.

***

Abby's fingers flew over the keyboard. Well, not literal flying, but her ideas definitely surpassed how quickly she could put them on the computer. In a rare pause, she glanced at Muse.

Muse's face contorted and moved through various expressions. Abby wondered how she had not noticed before how expressive Muse could be. Whenever something sparked her interest, Abby could see the delight spread across her face. Eyes crinkling, lips turning up, vigorously shaking her head. Actually, Abby had noticed. It was clear that although Muse had bluntly talked about her mother, she did not wish to delve too deeply into the subject. No matter how curious Abby was, she wouldn't go to a place that might cause pain. Maybe in time, she'd ask. Muse had a mother. That was big news.

At first, Abby had to suspend her burgeoning idea for a story in order to assist Muse with navigating the Internet on Abby's backup laptop. Muse's efforts were clumsy at first.

"Move the mouse to this little picture here." Abby put her hand on top of Muse's and helped guide her to Abby's preferred search engine. "Now, take your index finger and double click."

"Double click? How do I do that?"

"Just push that button twice real fast."

Muse tried, but nothing happened.

Abby laughed. "It takes practice. Try again."

Her mouse moved slightly off the icon, and when she clicked twice in rapid succession, nothing happened again.

"Arghhh. How come it was much easier to learn how to make love?"

"Try again, you managed to double click fast enough, but your mouse wasn't where it needed to be." Once again, she put her hand on Muse's and guided her to the icon. But this time, she also placed her own index finger over Muse's to help her double click.

The search engine opened, and Muse clapped her hands in delight. "I did it."

"Now, type in *lesbian sex*." Abby grinned.

"Naughty." Muse laughed.

"You still have a lot more to learn. There are endless possibilities, and we only tried a few."

Abby covered her mouth so she wouldn't laugh as Muse used her index finger to hunt and peck as she typed the letters into the area Abby had indicated.

Watching Muse poke at the keys, reading and reacting to what she was viewing, proved more entertaining than continuing to type Abby's own ideas. She'd come to the end of a scene a few minutes ago and wanted to give her brain a rest. Her exuberant expression was hard to ignore.

Muse must have felt her stare and looked up. "Are you on a break? I didn't want to disturb you, but this is so exciting."

Abby saved her draft and then closed her laptop. She snuggled next to Muse and looked over her shoulder. "Show me what's got you gyrating all over my couch in excitement."

"I think we may be over-inflating our usefulness. I typed in the word *inspiration* in that little box you showed me, and look what I found."

"Oh, those. Yeah, I've come across a few of those quotes but never seriously considered using any of them to jump-start my writing." Abby pulled at the hairs on her brow.

"Why not?"

Abby shrugged. "I guess they seem kind of cheesy to me and not all that helpful. I've been more successful after entering into social media discussions on topics that I'm interested in. I have to admit the two that mostly catch my eye these days are politics and sex. I can waste a lot of time with back-and-forth dialogue on either. There's a bunch of sites that address writer's block, too. Never helped one bit. Besides, if it were as simple as getting people to visit those sites, all inspiration would not have come to a screeching halt the last time you took a vacation."

Muse crinkled her nose. "Good point. But there simply has to be a way to use this particular tool to allow more efficiency."

"Too bad you can't have a nudge site. Maybe there is a way to have people go to the site, get your magic nudge, and go forth and produce. They'd have to be able to do that without requiring a more hands-on approach. Perhaps it can run independently."

"I wouldn't know where to start." Muse's shoulders sagged.

"I'd help you, but I have to admit, I don't understand the mechanics of how things work. That nudging thing was a bit fuzzy for me."

"It's a hard concept to wrap your arms around. I understand. I've been doing it so long, that it's second nature to me. But, if I try to explain how it works, things fall apart. Obviously, that's true by the look on your face earlier when I tried to tell you about my world. Your eyes glazed over."

"I kind of understand." Abby's head bobbed up and down.

Muse arched her eyebrow.

Abby laughed. "Okay, I don't get it. Not even one bit. I was trying to make you feel better."

"You should write a bit more, and I'm gonna try to figure this Internet out. There must be a way to harness the power."

"I think you should play around in the various Facebook groups. I can give you my login and password. I believe some writers have found it useful to commiserate with other authors when they've been creatively blocked. They join writing sprints, encourage each other, that kind of thing. It never worked for me. I usually felt more stress, not less. That's why I've never participated in NANO."

"NANO? What is that?"

"This thing that happens every November. You're supposed to write an entire novel in November. A minimum of fifty thousand words. I always thought I was killing it with a goal of a thousand words a day. The thought of writing nearly two thousand words each day had me blocked tighter than a clogged drain."

"I have enjoyed the few occasions where I've nudged someone to jump on Facebook, and then couldn't resist watching the back-and-forth dialogue. The groups for writers and readers are the most entertaining. I don't know if I should pretend to be you, though. I might feel compelled to join in, and that might get you in hot water."

Abby laughed. "Set up your own page."

Muse's eyes brightened in excitement. "Oh, could I? Will you show me how?"

"Sure. We need to establish an email address first, then we'll do a profile. Oh, I should take your picture to put on the profile. You'll be sure to get loads of friend requests when they see your gorgeous face."

"So, objectively, is my appearance pleasing to those who might wish to engage? I see people post a profile picture, and it's like an advertisement."

"Oh, yeah. It certainly is, but that isn't what makes you irresistible to me. It's your innocence and delight. I may not like the choice you made to return to wherever you went, but that also shows your kindness and consideration for something greater than your own needs. How could I fault you for that?"

Abby pointed to the screen on the old laptop. "Click on my email account."

Muse was getting the hang of the mouse and had quickly accessed Abby's email. "I don't understand why we need to open your email."

"You're going to add a new account." She pointed to the Add account box. "Now click there. You can use my phone number. It won't matter."

Muse and Abby spent the next fifteen minutes setting up a new email account and then a new Facebook page. After that was done, Abby suggested five of her favorite readers and writers' groups, and when Muse immersed herself in the vortex of social media, she returned to her new manuscript, inspired by a brand-new direction to take in the story.

***

Muse was so engrossed in her foray into social media, she hadn't noticed when something very monumental occurred. A short cough from Abby caused her to look up. Calli stood in Abby's living room with a smirk on her face.

"Oh, my, aren't you two the epitome of domestic bliss?" Calli swaggered forward and then plopped onto the chair. She leaned back and crossed her legs as if she didn't have a care in the world.

"I take it Zeus doesn't care anymore since I've let the cat out of the bag." Muse crinkled her nose and looked at Abby. "Have you ever researched that saying to know what it means?" She shook her head. "Never mind. Abby, meet Calli, my mentor, and all-around pain in the ass."

Calli wagged her finger. "After everything I've done for you. Have you forgotten that I was the one who went to bat for you and allowed this experimental time to see if we could consider alternatives to what has been tried and true for thousands of years? I should be very angry with you right now. It's one thing to spill the beans for one subject, but now the best friend knows."

"She needed someone to talk to. That's on me." Muse pointed to herself. "If I hadn't left, Jenny never would have known a thing."

"I thought Peter was supposed to help with that. Another rule you broke, and it didn't matter because she told the best friend, anyway." Calli shook her head in disgust.

Abby momentarily knit her brows together in confusion but then recovered and pivoted to Muse's mentor. "Oh, um, Calli, I'm delighted to meet you. Muse has told me about you. If you were the one responsible for this second chance for us, I don't know how I'll ever be able to thank you enough."

Muse was happy when Abby redirected the conversation. She chuckled inside at how her tactic of redirection had rubbed off on Abby. She would have to explain about Peter later because she had undoubtedly picked up on Abby's reaction to Calli's rebuke.

Calli shrugged. "Well, I didn't do it for you. You're not in my territory. I don't have to inspire you in any way, but this one moped around so badly, it was affecting everyone's mojo. Something had to give."

Hesitating to ask the question she desperately wanted to know the answer to, Muse skirted around the issue. "So, how ya been?"

Calli's face contorted. "I'm not going to lie. Zeus is not happy. Things are a bit rough. Nothing like what happened before, but it isn't optimal, Muse. I sure hope what you've been laboring on is a better solution than what we've put in place for the next three days."

"I'm working on it. You gave me three days, and it's barely been twenty-four hours. Why the absolute absence of patience? Hey, we" —Muse gestured between Abby and herself— "were talking earlier, and Abby wondered why we couldn't call upon another to take my place."

"The others are crying foul. I told you this might happen. Everyone but the ancients are asking why they can't take a holiday. Zeus is crabby listening to their grumblings. They're talking strike. One of them suggested forming a union. A union! Territory size and the number of subjects to manage were at the top of the list to negotiate about." Calli sighed.

Muse narrowed her eyes but decided to overlook Calli's blatant deflection of her question about training another. She would corner Calli later when Abby wasn't around. Perhaps this was secret Inspiration business, and talking so openly would only anger Zeus and the others.

"I want to find a way to telecommute because I've decided I'm not going back. I can't. I won't." Muse crossed her arms and glared at Calli.

"You're not?" Abby's eyes widened.

"Not if I can find a way to make things work. Why should you be any less important than my other subjects? Who says I need to sacrifice one for the many?"

"Zeus does," Calli yelled.

Abby took hold of Muse's hand and looked at her with unshed tears. "I don't want you to sacrifice anyone else for me. If we can't find a solution, I'll find a way to the other side of my despair."

"See, she understands what is at stake. Why can't you?" Calli challenged.

"Because I've fallen in love with Abby, and I can't go back to the way things were," Muse admitted.

"You have?" Abby blinked and searched Muse's eyes.

"Yes, I have fallen hopelessly in love with you, and nothing will change that." Muse placed a gentle kiss on Abby's lips.

Calli cleared her throat. "Have you forgotten I'm sitting here? I am not partial to voyeurism, so please stop with this lovey-dovey stuff. You love Abby and Abby loves you. I get it. Let's move on, okay? We need solutions, not declarations of undying love."

Muse sensed that Calli was trying to act gruff, but she'd seen the flash of emotion. It looked almost maternal. No one would tell her the story of her mother. She'd begged and pleaded, but Calli refused to budge, abruptly cutting off her questions. Calli had been her mentor, but more than that, she'd also acted like a mother.

"Is she correct? Do you love me too?"

Abby stroked Muse's cheek. "Of course I do, you goof. So much it hurts." Abby leaned in and kissed Muse for the second time since Calli had crashed the party.

Calli groaned. "Oh, for Pete's sake. Are we done yet?"

"You're just jealous," Muse mocked.

"Am not. Is this social media thingy going to work or not?" Calli had a definite, human-looking scowl on her face.

"I need to become more proficient, but I have an idea. If we can somehow capture the power behind these devices, perhaps we can expand our nudges through technology. It might not work with all artists, but it definitely has the potential with writers. Could we consider a restructure? Maybe create specialties and combine territories."

"I don't know if he'll go for that. Some may not prefer specialization. I know that I like the variety." Calli uncrossed her legs and leaned forward. "Hey…I was wondering," she hesitated. "Do you think I could try wine, chocolate, or maybe ice cream? I've always wanted to taste human food. Those three items seemed like a good place to start." Her expression was uncharacteristically sheepish as she made the request. "I never got the…" Calli stopped herself.

Muse was suddenly very curious about what Calli had almost revealed. The moment was quickly lost when Abby jumped in. Maybe Muse was more aware of human emotion since falling in love, or perhaps it was something else, but suddenly Muse spotted an odd phenomenon. Had Calli always been like this, and she never noticed?

"I recommend ice cream first," Abby offered.

"Oh, yes. Me too. Wine goes better with a meal. As a standalone, ice cream is preferable to me." Muse decided not to think too hard about how Calli might not be the hardass she'd always thought her mentor was.

"Um, I'm not interrupting your alone time, am I? You can always do that thing you did with each other after you go to bed, right?" Calli looked away in discomfort. Muse had never seen her so uncomfortable. It was almost like when humans had the sex talk with their children for the first time. Calli was acting very strange. Yes, very strange, indeed.

"You mean sex?" Muse asked.

"Making love," Abby corrected.

"Yeah, sorry." Muse screwed her face in apology.

"Well, yes, whatever else would I mean?" Calli gruffly responded.

"You are not joining in." Muse glared at her mentor.

Calli shuddered. "Ew, no."

"I do not engage in threesomes. Not that I think there is anything wrong with that," Abby quickly added. "Different strokes for different folks. No judgment here."

"I'm not interested in that." Muse looked lovingly at Abby and took her hand.

"The ice cream, please, before you get lovey-dovey again," Calli redirected.

CHAPTER THIRTEEN

Abby didn't quite know how to proceed with Muse after Calli had basically faded away. She wasn't sure why there was awkwardness between her and Muse now that they were getting ready for bed. Abby didn't specifically invite Muse into her bed. She didn't have to. It was implicit. But, was it assumed they would make love? Abby certainly hoped so. Unspoken words hung heavily in the air, thick like a November fog. She didn't like it one bit, just like she didn't appreciate it when she couldn't see more than a few feet of the road in front of her during those foggy mornings.

Both of them had easily uttered the L word without a bit of hesitancy. Why were things so uncomfortable now? Abby had to admit she had begun to cogitate about the possibility that Calli and the others were watching them. That thought was undoubtedly unsettling, and she wasn't sure if she should bring that into the open for them to talk about and dissect.

"I'm sorry for Calli's abrasive personality." Muse took a seat on the end of the bed with her hands clasped. "She's always been the type to keep her distance from her subjects. That doesn't make her any less effective. She just has a different style and hasn't had the same experience that I have. None of them have."

Abby sat next to Muse and took her hand. "I wasn't offended if that's what you think. But I have something to confess to you."

Muse brought her head up, and the question was written all over her face, but she remained quiet long enough for Abby to fill the void. Pushing ahead, Abby blurted her concern.

"Do they, I mean, your co-workers watch us?"

"It's complicated. No, they don't hover above a viewing device or anything. I don't quite know how to explain."

"Try, please."

"It's more like they are aware of what's happened. Have you ever heard the theory of genetic memory?"

Abby shook her head. "No, sorry. I've never heard about that."

"Some of my subjects believe a sort of memory exists at birth. Handed down over generations. The memory is encoded into the new person, based on common experiences. For example, the age-old fight or flight. Why are people afraid of certain animals they have never come across before? It goes all the way back to prehistoric times. The memory is just there. That's what it's like for us, the awareness is there, and it isn't concentrated on one subject. That's how we can inspire so many, all at the same time. It's a skill that is simply there."

"Okay, wow. I'm trying to wrap my head around all of this, but I guess I don't have a big enough brain. It's hard."

"Okay, how about religion or faith? You can't see, hear, or touch faith, but you have it. A lot of people don't question that. I can assure you it isn't like we're watching a square box that allows us to keep tabs on you. Push that image from your head that we're gathered around a kind of movie screening of your lives, complete with porno images." Muse laughed.

"How did you know that was exactly what I've been imagining?" Abby blushed.

"I just know." Muse kissed the tip of Abby's nose.

"So, Peter?" Abby shifted the conversation to the topic she'd been curious about since Calli had nonchalantly mentioned the kind old stranger who had introduced himself as Peter.

"About that. Well, I thought if I sent someone that reminded you of your father, it might help with my abrupt departure." Muse avoided looking Abby in the eye.

"Don't worry, I think that was sweet of you. I'm more freaked about this whole awareness thing and trying to wrap my head around that. Sending someone to ease my heartbreak doesn't even register on the discomfort meter." Abby brushed her fingers over Muse's cheek. She was doing her best to settle and let the flow of Muse's love envelop her. She was going to squander this opportunity to connect with the woman she loved if she wasn't able to let her unease dissipate.

***

Things were different this time around. Muse was being allowed vacation time as long as she agreed to continue to be Abby's inspiration. Another part of the deal was that Calli would continue to monitor Muse's progress. These had been easy stipulations to agree to. Now however, she recognized Abby's hesitancy to return to the same level of intimacy they'd explored the final night of her previous visit. Muse wasn't sure if she would be able to allay Abby's fears, and at this moment, she wasn't thrilled with Calli popping in and sparking Abby's current distress.

Muse desperately wanted to touch Abby but she was acting like a skittish kitten. Muse's heart ached with a craving she hadn't known before until she'd met Abby and fallen hopelessly in love.

"I don't want to assume anything, Abby, but I love you, and I want to touch you right now. I'm having difficulty not doing that, yet there is a kind of barrier between us now. I don't like this."

"Oh, Muse, I'm not conflicted about my desire for you. I have to get over this feeling that Calli is hovering above this bed, wanting to join in. My writer's imagination is too alive and well." A nervous chuckle escaped from Abby as she shifted on the bed.

"I assure you, that's not happening. Calli knows enough to stay clear. She got her sweet treat tonight. I think she's happy. May I kiss you properly now?"

Abby leaned into Muse, and Muse took that as her cue to close the gap and begin exploring Abby's eager lips. Of all the kinds of touch she had experienced before with Abby, Muse counted kissing right at the top. The feel of Abby's tongue and velvety soft lips never failed to send a jolt of desire to the place where moisture pooled whenever she thought of Abby touching her down there.

A soft moan erupted from Abby, and almost as if it were an automatic response, Abby's hands began to roam over Muse's back. They found their way to the edge of her shorts teasing the outer edge of the waistband. Muse couldn't take the anticipation much longer.

"I need to have your naked skin against my body," Muse pleaded.

In a flash, Abby removed her clothes and tossed them on the floor. Muse followed suit. They slammed together, kissing with the force of passion behind their movements. Muse pushed Abby onto the bed and climbed on top. She began to rock on top of Abby, and her excitement approached nearly frenzy levels as Abby met her every thrust. She punctuated her desire with a long, low moan.

Muse had an overwhelming need to feel the hot slickness she'd come to experience the last time they made love. Surrendering to that need, she slipped her hand between their naked bodies and sighed in satisfaction when she moved her fingers through Abby's folds. Her strokes were slow and deliberate. As the rhythm increased, Muse knew Abby was close.

"Please, don't stop." Abby's desperate plea came in a throaty whisper.

Finally, Muse felt Abby start to pulse as she slipped her finger inside. Muse didn't need for Abby to touch her as she rocked her center to the rhythm of Abby's orgasm and tumbled over in ecstasy two seconds after Abby's climax.

Abby sighed, and her body relaxed into the soft pillow-top mattress. "That was…oh, wow, so nice. I don't care anymore if the whole passel of Inspiration Specialists watches us."

"Inspiration Specialists?" Muse pushed aside a strand of hair and quirked her eyebrow.

"I don't quite know what to call you. Since you've never given yourself a title, I thought I would give one to you. Unlike Death, there are a lot of you, so I couldn't say I didn't care if Inspiration hovered over us. That would not be technically accurate."

"Good point. We've never given ourselves a title other than Inspiration Northwest or Inspiration Mexico. There is no title for the collective. Although, I don't think Calli will like being referred to as a specialist. She probably wants to be called something like executive or director. The others might feel the same. We're a haughty bunch at times. Especially the ancients."

"You don't seem haughty."

"I used to be."

"I don't believe you."

Muse shrugged. "I've mellowed over the years and been influenced by some of my nicer, more genuine subjects. I don't consider humility a weakness anymore. Besides, love tends to bring out the best in everyone. I highly recommend it for humans and specialists." Muse kissed the tip of Abby's nose.

"Well, you don't have to be humble about your, uh, lovemaking skills. You certainly are a fast learner."

***

"But I don't want to squander my short time with you by writing. It was a miracle I managed to get any work done yesterday." Abby bit the corner of her lip. "Can't we go back to bed now and forget work for a few days?"

Muse reclined on the sofa after their large breakfast of pancakes and mini turkey sausages. She shook her head, but her eyes and smile told a very different tale. The buzz of Abby's phone interrupted their conversation, and Abby glanced down to see who was calling. She should have known it was Jenny.

"I better answer my phone, or Jenny will continue to call. Or, worse yet, she'll drive over to check on me."

Muse offered Abby the thumbs-up gesture as Abby pressed the button to answer the call.

"Hey, Jenny."

"I think we should try a re-do for dinner. I know David would love to shove another stack of books under your nose to sign, and it will also give us a new opportunity to get to know Muse. I sensed she was not quite herself the last time she came for dinner." Jenny's voice was chipper on the other end.

Abby was concerned about how much Jenny might have shared with David and what Calli's reaction would be regarding the ever-expanding number of people in the know. She decided to nip that in the bud in case it wasn't already the runaway train she feared.

"We'll come, but only if you promise that this whole, um, situation, stays between us."

"Oh, don't worry about that. I like David, but I don't think he'd understand. Men are way too logical. Even though he is a pretty sensitive guy, I'd hate for him to think we're looney tunes. He already has theories about mass hysteria. You know Freud started that bullshit, and he directed his theories about mass hysteria onto women. He was such a misogynist pig. Penis envy, my ass."

Abby laughed. "Yes, I believe I can honestly state I'd never want that ugly thing dangling between my legs or anywhere near there. What time?"

"Come around six. That should give you two plenty of time to fuck each other's brains out."

Abby groaned. "Remind me why you're my best friend? Really, that's how you describe such a beautiful and intimate thing?"

"You're the writer, not me. See you tonight." Jenny's trailing laughter stopped when Abby ended the call.

"It's fine. I would enjoy having dinner with Jenny and David again. I'd like to redeem myself in their eyes. I didn't leave a positive impression the last time we joined them for dinner. David seems like an interesting person. If I can make things work, I'll need to converse with both Jenny and David without raising suspicion. This will be a good trial for me."

Abby ran her hand along Muse's inner thigh and lifted her eyes. She tried for her most seductive look. "Now, where were we?"

"You should be writing while you're on a roll. What better way to be inspired than having your own personal inspiration so close?"

"The only thing I'm inspired to do this morning is hop back into bed with you. You should know, inspiration can't be forced."

"True, we work through nudges. I should try to find something this morning that will nudge you to action. I've been reading in those writing groups, and it says that people can push through writer's block by simply writing anything. Even if the writer ends up deleting most of what they've written. Like exercising a muscle. Use it or lose it."

"That may work for some, but I've already told you, it doesn't work for me. And it doesn't work for a lot of others. If you've read the threads on writer's block, you would realize that. Come on, Muse, you know this."

Muse hung her head. "I do, and that's why I took a vacation. I felt so ineffective. My usual nudges were not working." She cupped her hand around her mouth and whispered, "I think they got worried this would spread. Like a disease. We'd become obsolete if our nudges no longer worked."

"I believe you might have to recognize that you can't control everything. Artists need to be in a particular space to be receptive to those nudges. I could write yesterday because I had a winning combination. You returned, and that put me in the right space to receive your nudge."

"Hmmm, I suppose you're correct. I never thought about it like that. I can't nudge an unwilling subject, so we're more partners than I think I realized. Thank you, Abby. You've given me an idea."

"How about if I inspire you in a completely different way? Come on, all work and no play…" Abby grabbed Muse and led her into the bedroom. She was grateful that it didn't take a lot to persuade her.

***

Calli approached Zeus with trepidation. His anger emerged in waves. The temperature in the space they both occupied had risen several degrees. "You were supposed to monitor the situation."

"I have been. Unfortunately, we're dealing with something entirely foreign. Neither of us can control Muse's emotions."

When he sighed loudly, Calli constrained her reaction. She didn't want to laugh, but everything about this situation pushed her newfound sense of humor. Rather than influencing Muse to step back in line, she had developed human reactions and emotions. Calli had to admit it wasn't the worst thing to happen to her.

"Give Inspiration Northwest an inch, and she galloped a mile. I should have expected this to happen. It runs in the family."

Calli nodded in agreement and smiled broadly. "Ah, yes, the other human saying is also applicable here."

"What is that saying?" His voice rose at the end, revealing his genuine interest.

"No good deed goes unpunished. You should never have agreed to my request all those years ago."

He chuckled. "You wore me down. You always were good with an argument. If I wanted to keep the peace, well, what choice did I have?"

"And, why can't you call her by her name? It's Musetta or Muse. You, of all people, should not insist on such formality. It may be time to release her and choose another." Calli wasn't sure this was the right answer either, but she'd been down this road before, and the solution had seemed so simple. She could feel her body slump as she thought of the prospect of revealing herself to Muse and sharing their family history.

"Will you tell her?" he asked.

"I don't know. What good will come of that?" Calli looked at Zeus, pleading with him to understand. Regret filled her soul and threatened to flow from her eyes in the form of very human tears.

"I wish you and your sister had chosen gods versus humans. I don't believe we would have faced these dilemmas. Sometimes I agree with your sisters. There is something inherently imperfect about the humans. Their seed travels through, appearing as a mutation far too often than

I'm comfortable with." He pursed his lips, and Calli felt a certain degree of anger at his apparent disgust.

"Are you serious? The Greek tragedies read like one of those cheesy telenovelas I apparently inspire in my subjects. The treachery of the original gods and goddesses was beyond atrocious. Yours included. Don't you dare sit on your high and mighty horse and preach that superiority to me. Have you forgotten about my mother?" Calli's voice rose in anger as she pointed at her boss.

"How dare you? My dalliances with humans have no relevance here. What has come over you? Have you forgotten how short my fuse is?"

Calli bowed. "I apologize. This whole situation is making me crazy. I only meant to point out that perhaps there is a double standard. Surely we can evolve as much as the humans with regard to this issue."

Raising his hands in supplication, he modulated his voice. "Fair assessment. You're right. I'll leave you to the ultimate decision, but you must make a new choice. Please choose wisely this time. Perhaps little Erato, she was named in honor of your favorite sister. I wish we had more time. She is not ready yet. This will cause havoc."

"Thank you for using her name. Progress might be slow, but I believe even a god can learn." Calli smirked.

Zeus shrugged. "Erato does not have a territory unless you wish me to call her Inspiration Backup." He laughed at his own joke.

"Honestly, I'm surprised she hasn't put together the clues. She knows my sisters and I are the original Inspiration. Like the other trained Inspirations, she must assume she is a descendant of the ancients. She doesn't remember Dumi, and for that, I'm thankful."

Zeus looked amused. "I must admit to finding that choice quite inventive. I don't remember you spending a lot of time in Africa to pick the name that means 'The Inspirer.' Who says gods or goddesses are not creative?" His look turned somber. "Calli, this is serious. We must find a resolution soon."

"Let me monitor the situation for the next two days. Perhaps it's salvageable. Who knew this internet thingy would take off like it has? Muse assured me there's a way to harness the power of the beast." Calli had relaxed her posture as her anger and irritation faded away. She had always been quick to anger when believing that justice was threatened, but angering Zeus was the last thing she should do.

"We did agree to three more days. I suppose we ought to let that play out."

Calli bowed her head. "Thank you. I'll also think about Erato. She is still young enough not to remember if we manage to groom her for a vacancy. I'm worried about pulling Erato so early as well. I agree with your assessment, but I believe it's an alternative worth considering."

"Ah, this is what they might call Plan B."

"Since when did you start to warm to the human sayings and other—"

"I could ask you the same question." He pointed to Calli. "Ice cream? Was it as good as they say it is?" Stroking his finely clipped beard, he smiled.

"It sure was," Calli responded.

***

Muse stretched her body as Abby continued to draw lazy circles on her belly. The contented smile on her face must have amused Abby, who laughed as Muse turned to face her.

"See, I told you I had mad inspiration skills. You haven't forgotten your idea, have you?" Abby asked.

Muse leaned in and placed a chaste kiss on Abby's lips. "On the contrary, you've helped to expand the notion. See, I never would have taken you for a woman who is so skilled with a toy. I suppose that's as surprising as Inspiration using different tools to enhance the experience."

"What do you mean?" Abby asked.

"I want to develop a website and call it *Nudge.* You gave me the original idea. It could be something new for people to latch onto. Connecting artists with one another. This seems to work well with other social media. Why can't it do the same thing for Inspiration? People love to connect with others across the net, so why wouldn't they seek Inspiration in the same fashion? I saw those other websites that are intended to inspire people, but they lack the magical energy I can provide."

Muse was so excited about her idea she failed to notice the doubt written on Abby's face.

"Social media is a necessary evil today, but that doesn't mean I have to like it. Now you're saying we'll have to depend on technology more than we are already forced to as a marketing tool. I didn't have a lot of skill with face-to-face interactions before, and that has only gotten worse." Abby sighed and linked her hands behind her head as she stared at the ceiling.

Muse deflated as the excitement whooshed from her body. "I don't know what else to do. If I can't find a way to amplify what I do, they won't let me stay. Calli wouldn't respond to my question about training another to take my place." A puff of air exploded from Muse's mouth in exasperation.

Abby turned to the side and pulled Muse close, stroking her back as Muse laid her head on Abby's shoulder. "It's just that it feels so fake sometimes. There is no way I have 3,000 real friends. Don't get me wrong, I have a lot of fun interacting, and people suck me in, but there's a barrier to true connection. On some level, I think that's why those websites have never worked for my colleagues or me. Deep down, I knew the inspiration came from somewhere else. Now I know it came from you."

Muse pulled away, leaving enough space to hold her attention. "I don't think you understand. The inspiration is always there, simmering below the surface. It's not something we give to you, but instead, we tease it with a nudge so that it rises with ease. I believe the missing piece is failing to understand there are times when no matter what nudges are offered, our subjects aren't prepared to accept them. Don't you see, if the *Nudge* site works properly, we'll be able to predict exactly when our subjects are ready to receive a nudge?"

"So, you only plan to use technology as a sort of predictor for perfect timing? You won't be replacing what you do with this Internet site? Okay, I think I kind of get it. The invention of the computer was merely a better tool than the typewriter or pen to put words on paper?"

"Yes!" Muse nodded enthusiastically. "I think it's about time to drag Inspiration into the twenty-first century. We're very old, antiques, really. And I'm counting myself in that descriptor, not just the ancients."

A tiny frown appeared on Abby's face. "I love technology, and it has definitely made my life easier, but one caution, faster and more efficient is not always better. Acrylic paints dry faster, but I don't think they can always compare to traditional oil paintings. Nothing is universal. Improvements, especially in the form of technology, have had unintentional consequences."

"Well then, perhaps we should have a tech-free evening?" Muse grinned.

"Are you kidding? Even if we started walking right this second, we wouldn't make it to Jenny's on time. We'll have to use my car. We can save the experiment for tomorrow. I'm game if you are. We can spend the whole day in bed. The only sacrifice will be cold coffee. I'll make a huge batch tonight to have in the morning."

"And, what shall we eat? No tech means you can't pull from a magic hat any processed foods. You'll get nothing from the refrigerator. No gas grills, either," Muse challenged.

"Fine, you win. I guess everything in moderation. A happy balance is the key. Maybe we should emerge from the bed and enjoy the beautiful sunshine and gifts from nature. There is nothing more inspiring than a long walk on the beach with the woman I love."

"The beach is magical to me. It's where I first saw you fall and spit sand like an Olympic Gold medalist—"

Abby shoved Muse and began laughing. "I'm not sure I like how I've introduced you to a certain type of humor."

"I like it very much, especially your laughter. I don't wish to see you cry like you did when I left. That's why this is so important to me. I have to try to make this work."

"I know. I can't believe I've been such a naysayer. Perhaps I'm afraid that if I don't poke holes in your plan, you won't develop a strong enough strategy to withstand the scrutiny of something I don't believe I'll ever completely understand. How Inspiration works is still a bit nebulous to me."

"You understand more than you think. Your holes, as you call them, reveal that insight."

***

Physically, Abby was still experiencing pain in her toe and tailbone as they made the thirty-minute drive to Jenny's house, but emotionally, she was flying high. Although it might have appeared that she was struggling, she felt like she had floated to the front door.

Jenny and David's twin smiles greeted Abby and Muse when the door opened. Abby was delighted to learn that Nat had decided to join the party, delaying the plans she had for later that evening.

"Enter. Hey, no wine?" Jenny mock scowled.

Abby blushed. "We sort of ran out of time and had to rush to get ready. There wasn't time to stop. I didn't think you wanted the open bottle. It's been sitting there for a while in the fridge. I should have poured it down the drain because that's how awful it was. But I didn't have the energy to do that."

"No, I certainly do not wish to drink your puke wine. Yuck. It was from a crap winery, too. It was undoubtedly a leftover from the dark time. Probably best to pour that shit down the drain. It's okay. I'm teasing. We have plenty. David always brings several over when he visits. You'd think he was trying to get me drunk and take advantage. Hon, there's no need to ply me with wine, you know I'm easy." Jenny cackled.

"Hey, not in front of someone who is still young and impressionable. Nat will think I've been a bad influence on you." David grinned.

"Oh, please. That acorn did not fall far from the tree. I've taught my daughter to own her sexuality. Nothing wrong with enjoying sex."

"Amen!" Nat appeared in the foyer. "Hey Aunt Abby and sexy Muse. Damn, if only I were ten years older."

"Shush." Abby poked Nat. "Quit being so impertinent and lusting after my date. David didn't even do that."

"That's 'cause he only has eyes for Mom. It's kinda sickening if you ask me, but at least she's getting some now. She could have before if she'd been more open to all the options. I'll bet you would have rocked her world. I heard lesbian sex is the best." Nat vibrated with energy.

"Git." Jenny pushed her daughter. "Go open a bottle of wine, and maybe I'll let you have a glass with us. I can't believe my baby is going off to college soon. I better demystify alcohol while I have a chance. David, give her a hand, okay?" Jenny turned to Muse and Abby. "Well, don't just stand there like bumps on a log, get your ass inside and give me an update on project Inspiration staying in Forks."

After Nat and David left the foyer, Abby whispered harshly in Jenny's ear, "Please tell me you didn't share what I told you with Nat or David."

Jenny pulled Abby into her home and whispered back, "Course I didn't. We'll talk in code, and they'll never know."

Abby groaned. "I'm not going to let you reread any of my spy novels. You think you're a badass covert agent."

Jenny laughed and then stared at Abby. "You look happy. Did you spend the entire day in bed?"

"What? No!" Abby shifted her gaze away from Jenny's scrutiny.

Jenny smacked Abby on the back. "You did too. You're such a liar and not a very good one. Is she good, Muse?" Jenny grinned.

"Don't answer that. Stop. Please. I need alcohol. Right this second. David," Abby called, "where is that wine? I need a glass, stat. I'm dying here."

Shortly after the trio settled into the living room, Nat returned with three glasses of wine precariously held between her hands. David was practically pulsating with energy as he held the other two, setting them down quickly in front of Muse and Abby. Nat approached her mother and let Jenny carefully grab two of the glasses, keeping one and setting the other one on the side table next to an overstuffed chair.

"I was wondering, Abby, would you mind signing the rest of my books?" David asked.

His smile was broad and genuine. When Abby coupled his enthusiasm with how gloriously happy she felt with Muse, it was hard not to match his grin.

"Hon, you should let them settle at least and have a few sips of wine before you pounce," Jenny chastised mildly.

David hung his head. "Sorry."

"It's okay, Jenno. I'd be honored to sign the rest of your books, David. It isn't often I come across such a rabid fan. You're going to make my head swell."

David bounded away.

"He's such a goof. But let me tell you"—Jenny cupped her hand against her mouth—"those surgeon hands of his are quite talented."

Nat scrunched her face. "Ew, stop, Mom. There's only so much openness I can tolerate. Let's violate Abby and Muse's privacy instead."

"Let's not, okay? Nat, are you excited to start college?" Abby asked.

"I am…" Hesitation leaked from Nat. "After we moved back here, I felt settled. Dad was such a dicknob, and I suppose I tend to equate larger cities with asshole fathers. I'm not sure I'll like living in a bigger place. That's a bit scary, I guess."

Jenny shook her head. "You shouldn't talk about your father that way. He loves you."

"No, he doesn't. I'm an inconvenience at best. I'm an adult now. You don't have to protect me anymore. I know the score. It's time to call it like I see it. The best thing that ever happened was you not insisting I spend any time with him and his new bimbo this summer."

David bounded into the room with an armful of books and looked at all the frowning faces. His smile fell quickly. "What did I miss?"

"Nothing, hon." Jenny sent David a look that Abby knew well. She was telegraphing to him that she would tell him later.

"I think it's cool that David loves your books. You know, you should be thanking me for that. I turned him on to you," Nat proudly announced.

Abby quirked her eyebrow. "You did, huh? Thanks, kiddo. Now can you spread the word to your thousands of friends?"

David set the books on the coffee table and presented a pen he'd pulled from his pocket. Abby began signing each one and placing them on the finished pile.

Muse absently caressed Abby's back as she made her way through the stack. Abby felt the warmth of her touch and glanced over to see the serenity and joy on her face.

"I'm sorry if I said something the other day that upset you, Muse. I'm so glad you agreed to have dinner with us. Jenny says that sometimes men are too stupid to know when they've stuck their foot in their mouth."

Muse chuckled. "Don't worry a thing about it. I was thinking about work too much. It was not your fault. Do you participate in social media, David? I was wondering if there are gender differences. For example, if you were a writer and, for some reason, you were stuck, would you go to a website for inspiration?"

David grabbed the glass of wine he'd set on the table earlier and took a seat on the empty chair. "Hmmm. That's a good question. I'm not sure since I can't relate to a block. I know I go on the medical sites when I require information. But I suspect that's very different. Don't throw eggs or tomatoes at me for saying this, but I don't think men gravitate to those touchy-feely websites littered with inspirational sayings. It's not how we roll."

Jenny raised her glass of wine in the air. "Hey, nobody is drinking this fine wine I paid a decent amount for. What do you need, a gold-plated invitation? That's my toast. Drink already." She clinked her glass with Abby and Muse when they picked up their glasses. The sharp ping startled David and Nat, who quickly followed suit.

"Thank you, David. The male perspective is critical, and something I hadn't considered."

"Why? Are you thinking of developing an inspiration website?" David asked.

"Maybe," Muse answered.

Jenny tilted her head in Muse's direction. "I think you should give it a try. Perhaps male artists are more sensitive. Doctors are notoriously nerdy and practical. Science and math, not art and literature, are at their core."

"Not true. I love literature." David pointed to the stack of books on the coffee table. "Case in point."

"That's only because you want to be a writer like Michael Crichton and make millions off a medical thriller. I love you, hon, but I don't think that's in the cards for you."

David pouted. "Fine. Maybe I don't have the writing skills, but I have killer…get it…pun intended…ideas. Abby could be my ghostwriter."

Abby shook her head and laughed. "Ah, now I get the real story. You're fawning over my books to get me to ghostwrite for you."

"No, no, I didn't…" David stuttered.

"Relax, David. I'm kidding," Abby interjected.

Abby noted Muse's momentary frown during the interchange before she plastered a quick smile on her face. Abby suspected David's adverse reaction to her idea was yet another torpedo to her plan. She vowed to be more supportive when they returned home. After all, her goals aligned perfectly with Muse's. Both women desperately wanted more time with one another beyond this additional three-day holiday.

Fortunately, the group quickly moved to other topics, and Muse was the perfect guest. She engaged with their hosts with ease and charm. Abby was able to sit back and enjoy the show as Muse completely enthralled them as much as she had done with Abby.

***

Muse had pushed from her mind the possibility her new website wouldn't work as she envisioned. It had to solve her dilemma. The alternative was simply not acceptable.

"I'm sorry for not being supportive before." Abby broke the silence in the car.

Muse reached over and laid her hand on Abby's knee, giving it a quick squeeze. "No, you're right to present reality to me. My influence is severely limited here. I'm not like Midas. I can't make everything I touch turn to inspiration, no matter how much I wish it were so. I understand it doesn't work like that."

Abby chuckled softly in the driver's seat as she glanced at Muse. "You talk as if Midas actually existed."

"Oh, he did," Muse acknowledged with a breezy casualness.

"Okay, wow. Did you know Midas? I enjoy Greek mythology like any other normal lesbian. I was, after all, addicted to Xena, Warrior Princess. Now, you're telling me, there may be truth to the myths?"

"Midas is not a myth." Muse crinkled her brow. "He was such an arrogant man. I get the impression we're descendants of gods and goddesses, but none of us are pure, similar to Hercules. His father was Zeus and his mother was Alcmene—a mortal. I guess you could say we're bi-deities— part human and part god or goddess. I suspect I am a descendant of one of the ancients, but I don't know which one."

Abby's eyes went wide. "I've been making love with a goddess? Do all of your sisters have a territory?"

Muse nodded. "Yes, of course. Everyone has a territory. It was a necessity as the number of artists grew, and we needed to split the territories in a different way. When I came of age, I was assigned to Calli. Some of my sisters were assigned to Calli as well, others to Erato.”

“Do you have any younger sisters who can take your place?” Abby asked.

Muse wrinkled her nose. “No, but there are young girls who I’ve seen hanging around Erato and Calli. I need to corner Calli…” Muse’s voice trailed off.

“Who is Erato?”

“She’s Inspiration Canada. One of the nicer ancients.”

“It’s kind of weird that you refer to yourselves as your territories. I don’t think it would resonate if I called out, ‘Oh, Inspiration Northwest, yes, right there’ while making love.” Abby giggled.

“No, that would not have the same impact, would it?” Muse laughed. “Zeus always liked to call us by our territory and only capitulated to using our names when he sensed a rebellion of sorts. I like my name.” Muse adjusted her body and sat up proudly.

“I like your name as well. It fits. Have you ever wondered about Calli? You said she is one of the original Inspirations. I’m a little rusty on Greek mythology. Let me type that name plus Greek mythology into Google. Knowledge is power. Your gift, like Midas’ touch, originated from somewhere, probably from one of the ancients. Maybe a search on the Internet will give us answers.”

“As with many gifts that are given, there is often a price to pay. Midas did not appreciate his gift when everything, including food and drink, turned to gold. Then and only then, did he wish to lose his gift.”

“If the price I have to pay for inspiration is that I won’t see you again…”

Muse's tear-filled eyes met Abby's. "I would have asked for the removal of the gift after my first visit if only the price affected me and me alone. I have to find another solution."

"I know. I don't need to return to my writing tomorrow. I need to help you. We'll find a solution together. This shouldn't fall completely on your shoulders. But you have to promise to let this go for tonight. You did a marvelous job at dinner. I swear that first thing tomorrow morning, we'll get on it. Tonight, you're all mine." Abby waggled her eyebrows.

"I can do that for you, sweet Abby. That will make it much easier to forget the urgency of the success of project Nudge." Muse once again made contact and ran her hand up Abby's leg.

"If you don't stop doing what you're doing, we might not make it home in one piece. Remember, for whatever reason, I am accident prone." Abby stopped Muse's teasing and moved Muse's hand back to Muse's lap. Abby playfully tapped her hand and said, "Stay. Don't venture outside of your own territory for the remainder of the drive. We can revisit this when we arrive home."

"I'm simply returning the favor from today when you kept me hostage for hours in the bedroom." Since Abby had awakened those very human feelings of arousal, Muse couldn't get enough of Abby, and it seemed likely that Abby felt the same even if she now kept Muse from bringing her pleasure again. The notion of there being a time and place for everything was proving challenging to adhere to.

"Are you complaining?" Abby asked.

"No, never." Muse grinned.

***

Zeus' booming voice filled the great hall, echoing loudly in the large space. "The time has come. I don't like hearing how the human plans to do research on us. Inspiration Northwest should never have mentioned Midas."

"With all due respect, *Father*, you're not absolved of all responsibility. Your propensity to spread your seed everywhere and have relations with humans has created havoc on multiple occasions. In human terms, she is your great-granddaughter." Calli had had enough of his arrogance and critical assessment of Muse. She only called him Father when she was especially irritated with him.

"You're teetering on the edge, Calli. You should think very carefully before opening your mouth again." He pointed his finger at Calli. "I'll allow a certain amount of grace, but tread lightly. I've no doubt Inspiration Northwest and her plaything will figure things out. What is written in their human stories is close enough to the truth to create an unnecessary disturbance. Thankfully, there are no stories of your daughter for them to discover." He sighed. "And yet I see an inevitable conclusion—like mother, like daughter. Erato may be our only choice. She seems more settled than Inspiration Northwest was at that age."

"That's because she has her mother, not another relative posing as a mentor," Calli argued with a touch of irritation in her voice.

Zeus raised his eyebrow. "Tomorrow, go to see Inspiration Northwest and tell her everything. Tell her of your daughter's choice and what became of her. She's entitled to know her fate should she choose the human. I believe, Calli, you have a bigger issue with that choice than I. Your sisters are irrelevant in this equation. Their haughty chatter is extraneous. Dumi did not produce an inferior daughter any more than you or Erato. Being a bit more human is not necessarily a bad thing. I only regret losing Inspiration Northwest. Until recently, she has done a fine job."

"Really, *Father*? I always thought you were disappointed with us. Mine was a foray into lust, but Erato, I think she really loved him. I should have supported her more. She had no one in her corner. Dumi was always so headstrong, and like Muse, she didn't require my acceptance to decide. I regret never having the chance to tell her I wasn't disappointed in her choice."

His eyes shone with rare softness. "You have the chance to do things differently this time around."

"I do. You aren't as cold and aloof as you would like us all to believe. Shall I also reveal who you are to Muse?"

"If you must." A tiny corner of his mouth lifted.

CHAPTER FOURTEEN

Abby rolled on her plush pillow-top mattress and patted the empty spot next to her. Her mood took an immediate downturn after expecting to connect with Muse. The area was cold to the touch, which indicated that Muse hadn't remained by her side for quite some time. Abruptly, she sat up, rubbing the sleep from her eyes.

Although her bladder screamed for release as the pressure built, she shuffled into the living room and found Muse focused intently on the laptop, typing as if she were part of an old school steno pool. Plato had curled next to her with his paw resting on her lap. Abby wondered how Muse could learn how to use the keyboard so quickly. Was this another skill attributable to her enhanced essence? Muse was something other than strictly human, so Abby supposed it made sense. She'd said she was part goddess or maybe something else? Abby didn't know, but it didn't matter because no matter what Muse was, Abby loved her. Even if she was unsure of so many other things, she wasn't uncertain of this.

"What time is it?" Abby's sleepy voice asked.

"Six, maybe six-thirty. You were sleeping so peacefully. I didn't wish to disturb you. It took time to create the website because the host wanted a credit card, and I didn't have a social security number to give them. So many levels of security to jump through. Frankly, it was very irritating. I had to use your cell phone to get a code." Muse was shaking her head and pursing her lips.

"So how did you get a credit card and social security number?"

Muse looked up from the screen. "This Google is addictive, but sometimes makes everything harder. I should have procured the credit card in the same manner as when I secured my motorcycle and clothing. I didn't need the social security number, birth date, and all the rest of that hooey."

"I don't understand."

"Never mind. Come, take a look. I've established many ways for artists to find *Nudge*. But I only have fifty-four followers." Muse frowned. "How do I get more people interested?"

Abby subtly crossed her legs as she remembered how much she needed to empty her bladder. "Give me a minute. I need to use the bathroom. I'll be right back, okay?"

Muse smiled. "You're doing that dance when you wait too long."

When Abby headed to the bathroom, Plato jumped from the couch. Like clockwork, he wove in and out of her legs while she sat on the toilet. Then he jumped onto the vanity, waiting for Abby to run the faucet and provide a fresh stream of water.

After emerging from the bathroom and heading to the kitchen in automatic mode, Abby filled the teapot with water. If she was going to start working so early in the morning, she needed coffee. Stat.

"Coffee first, and then I'll come to take a look at what you've done. What time did you get up? I didn't feel you leave the bed."

Muse swept her hair from her face. "I was in stealth mode. I didn't want to interrupt you when I felt the overwhelming compulsion to get this done. Time is running out."

Muse crossed one arm over her stomach and used her other arm to prop her head as she made a loose fist. The corner of her beautiful mouth settled on her hand as she stared at the laptop. She wasn't smiling. Reality hit Abby in the gut. If they couldn't get this working, their options were limited.

"I know, hon. I know. Do you mind if I conduct my own research on Greek mythology? Something is missing that I'd like to explore. I want to use the names you've given me. And, if you can think of more, that would help. There are Calli and Erato. Do you know the names of any of the other ancients?"

"Only one. Euterpe. She was usually pleasant to me. Her voice had this musical quality, and I remember following her around just to listen to her speak. The other six ancients were not very nice and could never be bothered to answer any of my questions."

Abby nodded as she removed the whistling tea kettle from the stove and poured the hot water into the French press. "That should be enough to start a search."

"Before you do that, can you help me entice more followers?"

Abby walked carefully to the couch and ran her hand down Muse's arm before sitting next to her. "I'm not sure how to help. Honestly, marketing has always been my weak point. I don't have many followers on my website or my author's page. Other writers I know swear by a mailing list, but you have to be able to give something away."

"I don't have anything tangible to give away." Muse frowned.

"No matter, it doesn't work for everyone. Hasn't worked very well for me. I've tried, only to discover that once a person gets the free story, they unsubscribe. Or worse, trash the story in a review." Abby shrugged. "Nowadays, if you aren't making bold racist, sexist, or homophobic statements, nobody cares. Seems like the people with the highest number of followers tend toward the negative. I know that isn't entirely true. I follow people with a moral compass pointing in the right direction." Abby waved her hands in the air, punctuating her words. "It does irk me when those outrageous posts get a lot of press. At least when something horrible goes viral, there is sufficient outrage to jar people into action."

Muse stared at Abby wide-eyed. "Um…"

Abby lifted her hand with her palm facing out. "Sorry, I just went down a huge rabbit hole. I'll get off my high horse. Try posting in the book groups. Post interesting tidbits or pictures of adorable kittens."

"I've noticed how talking animals are trendy. Shall I create a talking centaur? They aren't very cute, though. Minotaurs are worse—ghastly creatures and so foul-tempered. Don't get me started on sirens and harpies. Perhaps a talking mermaid?"

"Seriously? All those things are real? Didn't you have any cute, cuddly creatures? No pets? A talking mermaid might appeal to lesbians, but I think you want a broader audience." Abby grinned.

"Oh, I know. How about Pegasus? Horses are sometimes pets or faithful companions, right? Bonus that he can fly?" Muse's excitement nearly vibrated off her body.

Abby tapped her index finger against her mouth. "Maybe. That would be quite the hook. A talking Pegasus. Didn't he symbolize wisdom and fame? But where are you going to get an inspiring video of Pegasus?"

"I'll ask Calli. I wonder if Pegasus would mind? He has always been a friend to the ancients, but he was so earnest. I'm not sure about agreeing to a video."

"I thought Zeus transformed him into a constellation." Abby scrunched her face.

"That's only at night. During the day, he is free to roam."

"There is so much I don't understand and have to learn. You should see if Calli will help. I'm afraid I'm not adding any brilliance to the mix." Abby stood.

"Although Calli has been a good mentor, I've always felt like she's kept something from me. She tends to redirect the conversation when I ask too many questions. She's been doing that to me my whole life. Where do you think I learned that useful skill?"

"I'm going to see what I can ascertain from the bits of information you've provided and how they tie into mythology. I may not understand everything, but for some reason, I think there has been a planned evasiveness that could be an alternative to your website." Abby sat back on the couch and stroked Muse's face to soften the blow. "Just in case *Nudge* doesn't take off the way you want it to, the answer might lie in Calli's deliberate attempt to keep certain facts from you, and how she has ignored important questions."

"So, I'm not crazy. You noticed that, too?" Muse's brows furrowed.

Abby nodded. "I haven't had much contact with Calli, but yeah, she's a lot like you used to be." Abby emerged from the couch and went into the other room to retrieve her main laptop.

Muse returned her focus on the borrowed laptop, mumbling to herself, "Calli, what are you hiding?"

When Abby returned, she directed, "Skootch over, will ya? We can share this space, and if I find something, I'll show you. Okay?"

Muse moved a foot to the right, and Abby joined her on the couch, setting the laptop on her knees. Opening her favorite search engine, she typed in *Muse + Greek Mythology*." The first thing that sparked her interest was the *Nine Muses of Greek Mythology*.

"Oh, my Goddess," Abby declared and pointed to the screen. "Muse, look at this. I think the ancients are the nine muses. Apparently, Zeus did the horizontal mambo with someone named Mnemosyne for nine straight nights, resulting in nine babies, and a nymph I've never heard of, along with Apollo, raised them."

***

Muse didn't think it was such a remarkable discovery. She knew the ancients played a key role, and they were the nine muses. She was also aware of Zeus' many relationships with humans. She hadn't paid attention to the rumors that the ancients were his daughters because if she were a descendent of one of the ancients, that would mean she was related to Zeus.

"Is there anything about someone named Dumi?" Muse asked.

Abby typed on her laptop and shook her head. "No, other than it seems to be a name that means 'The Inspirer.' It's an African name. Have you ever been to Africa?"

Muse scratched her head. "No. I've only been here. Africa is a large territory."

"So is Mexico, but you said that Calli covers that entire country. Why?" Abby tried to understand the intricacies of how Inspiration worked, but nothing made sense to her.

"She's an ancient. They cover larger swaths than the rest of us." Muse yawned, and that reminded Abby she hadn't poured her coffee yet.

"I need coffee, and apparently, so do you." Abby shuffled into the kitchen and poured the coffee that had probably steeped too long into two cups. Focused entirely on adding creamer to both cups, she was startled to hear Calli's voice.

The casualness of Calli's previous appearance was missing. Her stiff movements and the straight line of her mouth denoted the seriousness of her visit as she sat on the empty chair.

"Hello, Muse. I believe I can fill in the missing information for you."

With a lifetime of training in polite behavior and a loss for what to say at the moment, Abby simply held up one of the cups. "Coffee?"

"Is it as tasty as ice cream?" Although the grim expression did not leave her face, the tension had lessened a tiny fraction.

"No, but if I put enough cream in the cup, it may come close." Abby added more creamer to one of the cups and brought it over to Calli. She set the other cup in front of Muse.

"Aren't you having some?" Muse's head tilted to the side.

"As soon as I heat more water, I will. My press only makes two cups. Don't let me interrupt. I think Calli was about to explain things, or should I call you Calliope?" Abby's eyes narrowed at Calli before she returned to the kitchen to fill the teakettle again.

Calli's protracted sigh filled the quiet in the room. "No, I prefer Calli. I might as well get the unpleasant confession out of the way. Dumi was your mother and my daughter."

"What?" Muse sputtered. "Then…you…you're my grandmother?" Muse squeezed her eyes shut before slowly opening them. Her voice cracked when she asked, "Why did you never tell me this before?"

Abby abruptly stopped what she was doing, and the teakettle banged loudly in the sink. The clatter caused enough of a distraction for Abby to cross the room quickly and sit beside Muse. She began rubbing Muse's back to settle her emotions.

Setting the coffee on the side table, Calli nervously rubbed her thighs. "You were young when Dumi made her choice. She was very spirited. The duty fell to me. We don't use terms like grandmother." A grimace appeared on Calli's beautiful face. "As the eldest living relative, I was assigned as your mentor. Sharing what happened to your mother might have placed undesirable ideas in your head."

"Like making a choice to leave?" Muse stood and began pacing the room. "Since I don't have an offspring to take over for me, what? I can't make the same choice? Is that what you're saying?"

"No…" Calli paused. "Not necessarily."

"What happened to my mother?"

"She lived out her life and grew old. She was not allowed to return, not even to see you. Her regrets were many. Not seeing you again or watching you grow was at the top of the list. He wouldn't let her take you." Calli's eyes shifted away.

Muse stopped pacing. The edge to her voice unsettled Abby. "He who?"

"The one who directs all of us. You know who."

"Well, he is not going to control my choices anymore. I'm not afraid of not returning, because honestly, I don't care if I never see any of you again. You are all dead to me. Problem solved. I'll remain here with Abby." Muse glanced quickly at Abby before returning her glare to Calli.

"Zeus is not one to anger. Don't be defiant, Muse. Making a choice to stay is one thing, but declaring your intentions with ire is quite another."

A loud boom reverberated through the house, shaking the foundation.

Abby's wide eyes shifted from Calli to Muse. "Was that Zeus? So, he's your father?" Abby turned briefly to Calli. "And what, also Muse's great grandfather? Holy shit, now that's a shocking pedigree."

Calli nodded and mouthed, *short fuse*, while cupping her hands around her mouth.

"Oh, this keeps getting better and better. Fine, tell me what I need to do to make this official. I would like to have an audience with Zeus and respectfully declare my choice." Muse looked to the ceiling.

"We'll go to see him together." Calli stood and held out her hand. "Muse, we must take our leave now."

Abby began to sweat as her breathing turned quick and shallow. "You'll be back?" As she stood, her body began to sway. She felt the blackness nearly overtake her senses until she felt Muse's gentle touch as her lover gathered Abby into her arms and kissed her.

"I will come back, I promise." With a final brush of her lips and caress to Abby's cheek, Muse stepped away.

Muse approached Calli, and the two disappeared in a mist after two short steps.

Abby blinked rapidly before the well of tears threatened release. Nausea quickly followed, and she stumbled into the bathroom, barely making it to the toilet. Zeus was indeed a vengeful god at times, and Abby knew he had the power to keep Muse away.

CHAPTER FIFTEEN

"Whoa, slow down." Jenny's voice sounded calm through the tiny speaker of Abby's smartphone. That was one thing she could always count on from Jenny. She had a level head and could talk Abby down from whatever cliff she'd climbed. Usually, those cliffs were related to believing she'd never write another book. Her career was over. They'd never been about a possible lost love.

"She's g-gone. She left with…with…Calli. Z-Zeus is angry. Thunder…bolt," Abby hiccupped between words.

"I'm coming over. Stay put and don't do anything stupid."

Abby slumped on the couch, setting the phone next to her. She continued to cry, and Plato jumped on her lap. She took deep breaths, and her tears began to subside as she stroked Plato's soft fur. At first, Abby avoided her laptop and the powerful craving to research everything written about the god, Zeus. She was scared to learn more, but she needed to know what she might be dealing with. Abby's burning eyes prompted a quick trip to her bathroom to remove her contacts and don her old-fashioned coke bottle eyeglasses before returning to the couch to begin her research.

Clinging to the promise Muse made, she grabbed her computer, and for the next thirty minutes, read about Zeus' most famed retributions against those who angered him. She shuddered as she learned of his intense cruelty. The sound of the key in her front door caused Abby to lift her blurry, red eyes in time to see Jenny enter.

Jenny did not waste time after gathering Abby into her arms. "Okay, now slowly tell me what's going on."

Abby concentrated on slowing her words. "Calli popped in and provided a shocking revelation to Muse about her mother and other things."

Jenny continued to let her arm drape over Abby in a comforting hold. "You need to take one more step back. Who is Calli?"

"Muse's mentor and grandmother."

"Shut the front door," Jenny exclaimed.

Abby sucked in a large amount of air and continued. "Guess who Muse's great grandfather is?"

"Hercules?" Jenny guessed.

"I wish. Nope. Zeus."

Jenny's eyes widened in disbelief. "Are you frickin' kidding? Zeus is a Greek god for shit's sake. Are you telling me those myths are real?"

Abby vigorously nodded. "Did you feel that shaking earlier? Like an earthquake after the loud boom?"

Jenny wrinkled her brow. "No, I don't know what you're talking about."

Abby pursed her lips. "Hmm, he must have directed his anger very specifically to my house. I've been reading about Zeus. He is not a nice god. Do you know what he did to Prometheus?"

"No clue."

"He chained him to a rock where an eagle pecked, or whatever eagles do, at his liver. That eagle would eat his liver every single night." Abby shuddered.

"If the eagle ate the liver, wouldn't that happen only once?"

"No, because he would grow back the liver. Ughhh."

"Okay, yeah, that's like creepy and overkill. I can't believe Muse, who is so lovely, is a descendant of Zeus."

"Yeah, and what he did to Ixion was just as brutal."

"I'm afraid to ask, but I'm so curious at the same time."

"He bound him to an eternally burning wheel." Abby grimaced.

"Now that's what I call extreme S & M. I don't suppose either was a willing participant."

"You're joking? Jenny, this is serious. Muse was a little defiant when she learned about Zeus, her grandmother, and her mother."

"Who's her mother? Xena, Warrior Princess?" Jenny grinned. "Probably where she gets her hotness from."

"Wrong again. There isn't anything about Dumi because, I think, she lived an unremarkable life once she decided to leave. They wouldn't let her come back to see Muse. That was a very steep price to pay, and I'm afraid of what Zeus will dictate."

"Okay, that's harsh, but not like the other things he did. Maybe he's less brutal with females or his own flesh and blood."

"He's not. He sent his mortal son, Tantalus, to the underworld and kept food and water just out of reach so that he would forever be hungry and thirsty."

"I never knew Zeus was so vicious. But all those examples are gods or men, right? Did he ever do anything to any of the goddesses or his daughters?"

"His wife, Hera, wasn't very nice either. When she found out her husband was dallying with Io, Zeus turned her into a cow and then gave her to Hera, who sent a gadfly to chase and sting her for eternity. I suppose, in Zeus' defense, he did try to sneak Io away from Hera, and that's why she sent the gadfly."

"How do you know all of this?" Jenny asked.

"I've been on the internet doing research. You live thirty minutes away. I had to do something to calm myself."

Jenny removed her arm from Abby's shoulder and pointed to the laptop. "That's not what I would label as calming. Research on all the punishments Muse's great grandfather doled out. Seriously, Abby?"

Abby dropped her hands in her lap and began using her left thumb to rub her palm. "I know, but research often settles me. Knowledge is power."

"How do you know that what you read is accurate? You don't believe every word in the Bible, do you?"

"No, but that's different. Mary Magdalene did not show up on my beach."

"Good point."

"I'm really worried. What if Zeus sends a crow to peck her eyes for all eternity?"

"He won't. He didn't do that with her mother. She doesn't have a child to keep her from, so no worries there. Calli doesn't sound like she's been very forthright, so keeping Muse from Calli won't hurt that much, will it?"

"I don't know. Calli and Muse seem to have an odd relationship. I think Muse does care about Calli and vice versa.” Abby leaned back and rested her head against the couch.

“What did she say before she left?”

“She promised me she would be back.” Abby turned her head to Jenny.

“Good, then trust her to keep that promise.”

“But at what cost?”

“I don’t know, Abby.” Jenny placed her arm over Abby’s shoulder and pulled her close until Abby rested her head against Jenny. Abby let the tears fall again. She couldn’t stop them. All she could do was wait.

***

Zeus sat on the enormous marble chair, looking every bit the supreme god that he was. In the past, Muse had only seen him in a more relaxed capacity. He was almost human in his manufactured presence. She wondered why Zeus bothered to deceive her. She hoped he didn’t possess the ability to read her thoughts. Calli had penetrated her frustration and anger, warning her that deference was the only option if she wished for a particular outcome. A quick peek at what Abby was researching about Zeus, and his propensity toward cruel and unusual punishments was enough to tamper her irritation.

Muse bowed her head. “I wish to present you with a request and offer my humble acceptance of your wisdom. Calliope has updated me on the price I must pay. I readily accept the conditions.”

Zeus tapped one of the stone armrests as his cold eyes surveyed Muse. “Inspiration Northwest, I applaud your ability to moderate your emotions. Earlier, you displayed the ill temper of your mother. What you ask will place a burden on the others and harm the region until we can train young Erato." His gaze pivoted to Calli. "What are your thoughts on her desire to remain with the human? Are you willing to mentor Erato and promote her before she is ready?"

"I'm prepared to do what is necessary, including going to my sisters to assist in the interim while I prepare a new Inspiration Northwest."

Calli continued to meet Zeus' gaze head-on. Muse thought this was a testament to her strength, and a renewed respect grew for her mentor even though Calli had not been forthcoming with their connection.

"Your existence will be finite, and you'll never see your sisters nor Calli again. Are you sure this is what you want?" He focused his attention on Muse again.

"Yes. I'll always feel my sisters, and perhaps Calli can use her skill to inspire me to make the website Nudge effective in the interim. Hopefully, that will lessen the burden."

Zeus grabbed his chin. "Hmmm. Very well. That's not the worst idea I've ever heard." He waved them away. "Make it so. I have other pressing issues to attend to, and this predicament has taken up far more of my time than it deserves."

"That's it? No fit of anger over my decision? How come you didn't let me do this the first time around? Why all the drama? From what I hear, your temper and punishments are legendary. I thought for sure you were going to tie me to a tree and let the seagulls poke out my eyes." Muse crossed her arms.

"If that's your desire." He pinned her with a stony glare, and she thought her insides might turn into snakes that would make their way through her digestive tract. She'd get a makeover like Medusa. Abby wouldn't welcome her new look, though.

"No, no. I appreciate this more magnanimous side. I'll be sure to correct the rumors. You clearly have gotten a bad rap over the years." Muse bowed and smiled.

"Clearly." He let the corners of his mouth turn up in a barely visible smirk. "I have one more condition…"

***

Jenny had closed Abby's laptop and refused to let her continue her obsessive search on every single spiteful punishment Zeus had doled out to anyone who dared cross him. At first, Abby resisted, but a walk on the beach had settled her raging nerves.

The dense fog kept the fatty water molecules floating in the air and added an extra dose to the already viscous mood. Abby shuffled her feet on the sand, dragging them along as if she were a toddler heading to bed too early for her liking. She wasn't paying attention when Jenny poked her in the rib with her elbow.

"What?" Abby turned her head and glowered at Jenny.

"Put your glasses on and look over there." Jenny pointed to the blurry outline of a woman walking in their direction.

Pulling the thick black-rimmed glasses from where she'd settled them on her silver necklace, joy flooded Abby at the sight before her.

"Don't run. I'll be by your side soon enough. I don't think you'll survive another face-plant, and I'd rather not glue your head again." Muse's smile shone through the thick mist of the morning.

Abby heeded Muse's warning but decided she could pick up her pace without tripping on a beach obstacle. In her more cynical moments, she wondered if a gremlin put them in her path specifically to mess with her. Muse had her arms open and waiting as she continued walking toward Abby.

The only thing Abby saw in front of her was pure love reflected in Muse's bright eyes. Beacons for her to get lost in. Unfortunately, those beacons kept her from carefully navigating the beach, and like so many other times before, she found the one item that would trip her. Spitting sand for probably the hundredth time in her life, she heard the musical laughter of Muse and the raucous mirth from her best friend.

"You put that log right there on purpose," Abby joked. "Will you kiss me if I have a mouth full of sand?"

"I'd kiss you with a mouthful of scorpions. The question is, would you do the same?" Muse offered her hand.

"Is that a new form of punishment from Zeus? Is he going to ruin our chance of being together?" Abby spit more remnants of the wet sand. "I knew it. I've been reading about his punishments. I wondered what terrible place he'd chained you to."

Muse gently brushed seaweed and debris from Abby's sweats and leaned in to kiss her. "Are you hurt?"

Abby shook her head and brushed her hand over Muse's cheek. "You're here. What does that mean? How long do you have?" She was afraid of the answer. These short visits were killing her.

"I'm here for as long as you'll have me." Muse smiled.

Abby narrowed her eyes. "What's the catch? What punishment will we have to endure? Will he really put scorpions in your mouth?"

"No, of course not. Zeus is my great grandfather. Why would he do that?"

"Um, Tantalus, who he sent to Hades, was his mortal son. Food and water was kept from his reach for all eternity. Oh, and Io, his mistress, was turned into a cow, have you forgotten about her?" Abby furrowed her brow.

"In all fairness, he only turned Io into a cow to hide her from Hera, and he tried to sneak her away after Hera found out. As for Tantalus, he deserved everything he got. Not only did he steal ambrosia from the gods, but he cut his son, Pelops, into pieces and served him to the gods. Now, I call that truly barbaric. Fortunately, they knew about it, and only one god took a bite. They brought the poor kid back to life." Muse answered as if those facts were evident to all.

"Please tell me you don't have any of these crazy tendencies toward retribution if anyone crosses your path."

"Oh, goodness, no. Our job has only been to inspire. We have never doled out justice. That's left to the gods and, on occasion, goddesses. Honestly, you have nothing to worry about. I've only given up my immortality and ability to interact with my sisters or grandmother. I will miss them, but it was nothing compared to the ache of never seeing you again. It's a sacrifice I'm willing to make." Muse cocked her head and glanced to her left. A serene smile formed on her lips.

"What just happened?" Abby asked.

"I'll tell you later." Muse focused on Jenny, who had hovered a few feet away. "Hello, Jenny. Thank you for taking care of Abby while I resolved my dilemma. I look forward to more dinners with you and David now that I have more time on my hands." Muse crinkled her nose. "I'll need to find something to occupy my days. Idleness is not an option. I'll continue to work on Nudge, but surely that won't occupy enough of my time to keep me out of Abby's hair while she writes."

"We thought you might be an editor. Do you think that's something you can do?" Jenny asked.

"Oh, no, I don't possess those skills. I only know when something is not right, and then I've nudged my subjects to take a different path."

"Art critic? Movie critic? Book reviewer?" Jenny tossed out the suggestions.

"I wish to make my own way. Could I make a living doing this?" As if something distasteful suddenly occurred to Muse, her face distorted into a grimace. "I had not considered the burden I would be placing on Abby."

Abby pulled Muse into an embrace. "Don't say that. Don't ever say that. I have plenty of money for both of us. The sacrifice you made is more than I could have hoped for. I love you, and I don't have any doubt you'll continue to be my inspiration. If you need another job, so be it, but why can't you consider your primary purpose as my own personal burst of daily inspiration?"

"Really?" Muse looked so hopeful.

"Absolutely. I think my best book is yet to come. With all of your energy focused on me, how can I possibly not succeed?"

"I'm gonna shove off. Okay? I think it's time to let you two reacquaint with one another and have mind-blowing sex." Jenny patted Abby's arm. "I want to hear all the details later."

Abby snorted. "No way. You had your chance to learn about the joys of lesbian sex first hand, and you passed on my offer. You'll simply have to continue to read my books, and maybe I'll base a future scene on my adventures with Muse."

"Fine. Kill all my joy. I guess I'll have to watch lesbian porn with David instead."

Abby plugged her ears. "Ew, don't say another word. The visual I'm getting is bad enough. You know that most of the lesbian porn is not authentic?"

"Really?"

Abby shoved her best friend. "Yes, really. I'll try to think of a movie that you can watch for a more accurate portrayal, but it isn't about porn. Mostly it's about intense emotion coupled with terrific physical sensations that only another woman can offer because a woman is best equipped to understand another woman's body."

"That sounds so hot. Damn, I wish I had a smidgen of bisexual inside me."

"The fact that you said that sounds hot probably means you do." Abby laughed.

"Not enough to have ruined our friendship. Now go have hot lesbian sex with Muse." Jenny turned and slowly made her way to Abby's house, waving and grinning as she walked.

***

One of Muse's favorite things to do was hold hands. She reached for Abby's hand and intertwined her fingers with Abby's. Her hand molded to Abby's in a perfect fit. Their joining made sense, and Muse noted how much they fit. Everything about how they came together was seamless.

"Before we go inside and I ravage your body, I want to know about that momentary distraction on the beach. You said you would tell me later." Abby tugged on Muse's hand.

"Calli. She whispered in my ear. I don't think she's ready to let go. Somehow, she's going to find a way to keep tabs on me. I don't think she got over the loss when my mother, Dumi, left. I don't remember her. I wish I did. I think I'm a lot like her. At least that's what Zeus said. I don't think he meant it as a compliment."

"Well, if she was anything like you, I would consider it the ultimate praise. I don't know Calli that well, but I'm willing to lay down a wager she's also a bit more like you and Dumi than either she or Zeus will admit to. Did she have a human lover, too?"

"I think so." Muse let herself be guided into the bedroom and sat on the edge of the bed with Abby. "I don't think they had ice cream when Calli took her jaunt on the wild side. Maybe that's the only reason she wants to keep tabs on me. She said ice cream was almost as good as ambrosia."

"Yeah, us regular old humans do some things right."

Muse brushed a speck of sand from Abby's cheek. "Um, you still have a few remnants from your trip on the beach."

"I should take a shower and brush my teeth. Goodness knows what germs reside in the sand. Scorpions are not commonplace in the Pacific Northwest, but there are a lot of other microscopic creatures that I'd prefer not to ingest or infect you with."

"Can I join you?" Muse blushed. "I've only read about taking a shower with someone. I wish to experience that joy."

Abby laughed. "Yeah, there's nothing quite like soaping a partner or relaxing in a jacuzzi with bubbles all around you and the aroma of lavender. That's my favorite bubble bath."

Muse bounced on the bed. "Oh yes, can we try that sometime?"

"I haven't used my bathtub in forever." Abby grabbed Muse and pulled her to a standing position. "No time like the present."

"I am so excited for this new experience." After following Abby into the bathroom, Muse retrieved her extra toothbrush when Abby pointed to the drawer. Abby hadn't tossed away her toothbrush, and Muse was touched by this small detail.

"I'll fill the bath if you want to brush your teeth." Abby turned the faucets on the large, heart-shaped tub that was surrounded by marble tiles. A waterfall spilled into the tub from a brass fixture. Abby then grabbed the purple bottle sitting in the corner and poured a healthy amount into the bath. The bubbles began to multiply on their own, and Muse detected the subtle hint of lavender. She breathed in the sweet smell and smiled.

As the water rose in the tub, Abby turned her attention to the sink and picked up the electric toothbrush, adding a small amount of toothpaste. The hum of the motor filled the room after Abby pressed the button, moving the vibrating brush in her mouth. The simple domesticity of this moment created such a warm feeling for Muse. She finally understood how comforting it felt to join in a kind of daily ritual with another person. She smiled as she watched Abby brushing her teeth. She could get used to this.

Muse wasn't shy about removing her clothes after finishing her quick brush. She sucked in air and felt the clean, fresh, hint of mint on her teeth. Muse loved that feeling, and in the short time she'd spent in Abby's house, Muse had looked forward to that human ritual in the morning. She had wondered about the electric toothbrush but was satisfied with the manual one.

"Do you think that one day, I could try that vibrator?" Muse pointed to Abby's electric toothbrush.

Abby pushed the button to stop the vibrations and laughed. "It's not a vibrator, but yes, I have an extra head I can switch out for you." She covered her mouth and began to laugh and a spray of minty foam escaped before she spit into the sink. "Oh. My. Goddess. Switching out a head? What kind of lesbian am I? Vibrators and heads? I think I have sex on the brain."

"That would be fun. Can we try a vibrator, too? Not the teeth-cleaning kind."

Abby nodded. "I think I knew what kind of vibrator you were referring to. Sure, there's a whole lot more I can introduce you to. I'm sure I'll have loads of fun being your mentor. Mmhm, a sex mentor. Now that is a job that might be more fun than writing."

"You can't give up writing to teach me these sex things. I can always do research. Is that not what you do when you need to learn about something. I found a video on YouTube on how to ride a motorcycle. I'm sure I can find videos on vibrators."

"I knew it. You had no idea how to ride, did you? Why in the world did you choose a motorcycle? An automatic car would have been easier."

"Ah, yes, but not as sexy and fun." Muse pointed to the bath. "I think that's about to flow over. I'll turn the dials while you get naked." She grinned and waggled her eyebrows.

Muse dipped her hand into the soapy water and swirled it around. "It's very warm."

Abby had finished pushing down her sweatpants and removing her socks. "Don't worry, your body will get used to it quickly. I didn't want the water to turn cold, so I may have made it a tad too hot."

Muse stepped into the tub and slowly lowered her body. "Ooh, ooh, hot, hot."

Abby laughed and dipped one of her toes into the suds. "It's not that hot, you big baby." After she stepped fully inside and positioned herself behind Muse, she exclaimed, "Yikes. Okay, maybe we should add a tiny bit of cold to the water." She turned the cold faucet on for a few seconds. "Ahhhh, that's better." Reaching for Muse, she pulled her close until Muse's back molded against her chest and stomach. Pushing aside Muse's golden hair, she kissed her neck. The long strands dipped into the water, causing the tips to drip.

Abby's hands began to move over Muse's breasts, and Muse sighed in contentment. When one hand landed between her thighs and Abby began to make slow circles on her clit, Muse arched a little to increase the pressure. Abby took her time, even though Muse kept lifting her rear, giving a silent hint to increase the speed and force. Abby refused to comply.

"Abby, oh, this is slow torture."

Muse could feel Abby's smile against her neck. "I know, but it's the best kind. Relax and enjoy."

"I am, I am," Muse's response came in puffs of air as her heart rate increased. She felt the building sensation as Abby continued to stroke her sensitive center. The warm water kept her body in a protective coating, and although she could feel the increase in temperature, the sensation building overpowered her other senses.

Higher and higher Abby took her, until the flood of feeling flowed, and Muse felt herself pulse against the warm water. Abby slowed the movement of her hand but kept her palm against Muse's clit until the contractions ceased.

"I like bubble baths," Muse exclaimed. "Shall we switch places?"

"No, stay right where you are, and I'll wash your back."

***

The tips of Muse's fingers continued to run along Abby's arm, hip, and buttocks as Abby and Muse faced one another. After their long bath, from which they finally had to emerge after running out of hot water, they'd taken their lovemaking to the bedroom. Abby couldn't remember ever feeling so satisfied and complete with anyone else.

For a brief moment, she wondered if this was a dream, and she would wake up suddenly. During those times when she'd wake from a vivid dream, Abby would grab the notebook she kept on her nightstand and write down everything she remembered. Those dreams always led to the start of a new novel. As Abby felt the heaviness on her eyes, she finally succumbed to sleep and entered into dreamland.

***

When Abby felt the soft caress to her cheek and a chill traveled across her body, she jerked awake.

"Are you injured?" Muse's velvety voice asked. It was the same calming quality she was used to hearing.

Abby quickly stood, brushing the sand from her clothes. She pushed aside her long hair that had fallen across her face. Muse's head cocked slightly to the side.

"Oh yeah, yeah. I fall all the time. I'm like the Olympic Gold favorite in the *falling-on-sand* sport." Groaning at her inane response, she failed to resist adding a ridiculous question to the end of the first words from her mouth. "Aren't you cold?"

This can't be happening. I'm talking to Muse, but it's like déjà vu.

The woman's mirth appeared on her face as a smile tugged ever so slowly at the corners of her naturally red lips. "Isn't this a beach? I have a swimming robe."

"Huh? Swimming robe? I suppose that's a good descriptor." Continuing to hold her hair away from her face, Abby squinted into the bright sun. "Um, we're not exactly on a beach in Southern California." Forging ahead, she added, "No, no, it was not a dream. Your name is Muse, and I know you. We're in love. Please, don't erase my memories." Abby looked to the sky. "I won't let you do this to us."

Muse's delicate laughter, fragile and beautiful like the wings of a butterfly, broke her silent chastising.

"I told Calli it wouldn't work. Love is far too strong to allow the magic of wiping a memory to take hold." Muse turned her head and spied Calli, who sauntered toward the women. "What will you do now?"

Calli shrugged. "Accept defeat, thank Aphrodite, and ask her to speak with Zeus. She's the only one who can get through to him sometimes. I tried to tell him that wiping your memory wouldn't work."

Muse turned her attention to Abby. "Hello, Abigail Prentice. I'm very sorry, but I needed this vacation to last a lifetime, and Calli said this was the only way he would allow it."

Abby's nose wrinkled. "Hmm, clearly you've never vacationed this far north. My place is within walking distance. Come with me. Perhaps a nice hot tea or cocoa will warm you up. Oh, and by the way, I plan on serving cocoa or tea for the rest of our lives. Because this vacation will definitely last a lifetime if I have anything to say on the matter." Puffing her cheeks and shaking her head, she looked into the beautiful blue eyes of her lover, confident in the assessment that this was not a dream.

"I wish to try this cocoa. That would be lovely. Thank you, Abigail Prentice, writer. And I wholeheartedly accept the lifetime of hospitality you offer." Muse brushed her hand against Abby's cheek and leaned in to kiss her. "Sand, yuck. Not this again."

"Another bath?"

"Oh, yes, another bath along with the cocoa would be a dream come true." Muse winked.

"And what comes after the bath? Shall we repeat that as well?"

"I guess there are advantages to Calli interfering and trying to wipe your memory of me. You know, I was supposed to try and seduce you again and get you to fall in love with me as fully human."

"Just to let you know, that would not have been hard. But I'm glad I remembered. Even the pain of separation was worth it. I'll cherish you more, knowing the pain of loss. Sometimes, we don't truly know what we have until we risk losing it. I could never forget that."

"Nor I. That made my decision so easy. I'm not giving up anything. I'm gaining something so precious that I'll spend a lifetime thanking Zeus, Calli, and Aphrodite for the gift before me. I love you so much." Muse kissed Abby again despite the remnants of sand that stubbornly refused to go away.

"Me too. Waking next to you every day until we pass over is an experience I'll never tire of. Knowing this wasn't a dream, and tomorrow I'll wake with you by my side, is the best gift any god or goddess could ever bestow on me." Looking to the sky, Abby brought her hands together and whispered, "Thank you."

A blink of darkness and then lightning flashed across the sky, followed almost instantaneously by a return of the glorious blue sky and sunshine. Zeus had apparently given a sign of his approval.

EPILOGUE

Little Erato rushed to visit Calliope and tell her what she'd learned about the writer, Abigail Prentice. She wondered if perhaps her mentor already knew when she saw the tiny smile on Calliope's face.

"Calliope, have you heard?" Erato asked.

"I have. Nice work, Erato. Although, in this instance, I believe the bulk of the inspiration came from Abby's personal experience with Muse. I'm glad her new book won't cause ripples with the other Inspirations. Apparently, being a bit more transparent was all they really wanted. Who knew that most are a sucker for a good love story?"

Calli lifted the paperback from her marble table and held it out for Erato to inspect. The inside cover of *Inspiration Takes a Vacation* contained Abby's loopy handwriting.

"Oooh, Abby inscribed your copy. Do you think she would sign one for me? I'm in her dedication, you know, along with you and Zeus. Wasn't that nice of her?" Little Erato ran her fingers across the script.

"I'm sure she will. Next time I go for my monthly ice cream, I'll ask," Calli answered. She was happy that Zeus had softened his judgment that Muse could never see her grandmother again.

"If I promise not to fall in love with a human, do you think Zeus would let me take a short holiday and taste ice cream?"

"Maybe, we'll see."

About the Author

Annette is an award-winning author, published by Affinity Rainbow Publications, Stone Soup Community Press, and now, Crazy Cat Lady Press, who lives in the beautiful Pacific Northwest with her wife and their five furry kids. With twenty-one published novels and the Goldie Award for her fourth novel, *Locked Inside,* she finally feels like a real author. Annette is as much a reader as a writer and is always looking for the next lesfic novel to queue up. She came up with the One Fan at a Time tagline because it rolled off the tongue much better than One Reader at a Time. After pondering who she was at her core, she found it was all about connecting to each reader on a personal level. Annette would be the first to admit she doesn't do well with the masses. If someone picks up her book, and it touches them, she believes she has achieved what she wants with her writing. Drop her a line. She loves to hear from readers.

Email: annettemori0859@gmail.com

Sign up for her mailing list: http://eepurl.com/cS7nr9

Check out her blog: Everyday Occurrences

https://annettemori0859.wordpress.com/

Note from the Author: Reviews make a huge difference in exposure, so if you liked this book or any of my other books, I'd be delighted if you took the time to write a quick review on Amazon or Goodreads. Many thanks!

Other Books from Annette

One Shot at Love

Blair returns to her hometown after the death of her sister. She's always been an activist, but this time she vows to use her voice to advocate for better gun control. At her lowest point, she meets Maribel, an irresistible, sexy woman who proves to be an enigma to Blair. Maribel can't help approaching the weeping woman. When she learns the origin of her grief, Maribel thinks she is the last person who should form a friendship with Blair. Ultimately, the allure is too much for Maribel, but how long can she keep her secret and continue to nurture their burgeoning feelings for one another. A committed left-wing social activist could never fall for the poster child of the NRA. Unless taking that one shot at love matters more than anything else.

Heart Strings Attached – Co-written with Ali Spooner

Socialite Remy has her world shaken, causing her to reevaluate her priorities. Bartender Chancy has her orderly life turned around when she is in an accident leaving her with no transportation. When a mutually beneficial business agreement between Remy and Chancy turns into undeniable attraction, will the two ignore culture norms to explore their intense desire for each other? Follow Remy and Chancy as they join the characters of the Trophy Wives Club and Pleasure Workers in a continued journey of love and exploration. Is love possible when women from two distinctly different social tracks are brought together by fate?

The Panty Thief

Joey Hartford is a fourth-year medical student who often jokes about her jealous mistress—medical school. She insists she doesn't have time for a relationship given the disastrous consequence of a diversion from her studies, but the new tenant in her apartment building is proving too tempting to ignore. Sabrina is also in her final year of her doctoral program. Her focus is on completing her dissertation for a topic she has long lost her passion for. Meeting Joey is dangerous for so many reasons. She should know, because mental health is her specialty? Add to the mix a suicidal ex-girlfriend who suddenly reappears in Sabrina's life along with Joey's jealous *friend-with-benefits*, and things can't help but get complicated quickly. Find out what happens in this humorous contemporary romance from award-winning Affinity Rainbow Publications author, Annette Mori.

Pleasure Workers

Alex Cortez is accomplished at two things, fixing broken equipment and pleasuring women. She is happily doing both at the Ranch in Nevada. Danna Nichols, newly widowed, feels lost and alone. When her good friend Lindy invites her to check out the newly established Trophy Wives Club, it awakens dormant feelings and desires. An instant attraction happens and the two form a bond under unlikely circumstances. Will the challenges of their social status tear them apart before they can enjoy the pleasures of their new love?

Compound Interest – Lesfic Bard Finalist

The kick-ass women in The Organization are back and they have their sights set on a few new recruits. Not everyone is jumping for joy at the choices, considering subterfuge is front and center in the games the new recruits have been playing. Dani is supposed to get her happily ever after, but she's not sure what's real anymore including Candy's feelings for her. When a new enemy takes Candy captive, Dani vows to uncover the truth by insisting on going on the mission to save her. Candy is not what she seems, and that presents a new set of complications for Dani and her feelings. The Organization continues to have challenges when those damn book magicians and book witches keep popping back in to warn them of new catastrophes on the horizon. She doesn't have time for their warnings until their enemies intersect once again to keep them working together. From award-winning author, Annette Mori, find out what happens in the final chapter of the combined Asset Management/Book Addict series.

A Window to Love – Lesfic Bard Winner

Two life events, two paths colliding, two souls destined to meet. Mandie Carter lives an uninspired life. No passion, no romance, and just when she thought things couldn't get worse, life throws her a curve. Gail Forrester is barely hanging on. Buried under mountains of debt, only her much in demand architectural designs keep her afloat. Now, they must find a way forward together through what life and destiny have in store for them. Only then can they hope to step into that window to love.

Unconventional Lovers – Lesfic Bard Finalist

Bri and Siera are young women with huge hearts and strong wills. They want nothing more than to find a peaceful and secure space to be, a place that fulfills their needs and gives them the freedom to be themselves. But the world is a harsh place for anyone who is different. Bri's Aunt Olivia is a vet with a thriving practice. She is set in her ways, single and surviving, channeling her emotions into her work and her love of Bri. Siera has a supportive but silent father, an overpowering helicopter mom, plus her Aunt Deb, who adores her. Despite their individual battles against hurt, prejudice, and rejection, can these four women find love against the odds?

Locked Inside – Goldie Winner

How much does the power of love matter to someone who has overcome obstacles greater than most people face in a lifetime? Carly, a beautiful and vivacious young woman, sees something in the semi-comatose Belinda, and they form an unusual bond. Can Carly help Belinda break free from her emotional prison? Will Belinda's fears allow their relationship to evolve into something deeper? Find out in this wonderfully evocative romance that is sure to touch your heart.